A NIGHT OF LOVE

By

José F. Nodar

Northport Booksellers / Spring Farm NSW Australia

Spring Farm NSW Australia / José F. Nodar First Edition

ISBN 978-1-7640642-2-4 – Paperback

ISBN 978-1-7640642-3-1 – E-pub

ISBN 978-1-7640642-4-8 – Audiobook

Table of Contents

For Miriam,

Anna,

Elizabeth,

Allison,

Mark,

Rachel

David,

and

Andrea.

You are always in my thoughts.

A Chance Encounter

Daniel

If I had a dollar for every time Ryan Michaels dragged me to one of these things, I could buy this entire café and convert it into a quiet bookstore—one where no one insisted on an open mic poetry night or clapped dramatically at metaphors about broken teacups.

Still, here I was again, sitting on a velvety stool that was too plush to be practical, staring into a lukewarm cappuccino and trying to pretend I wasn't counting how long I could stay before it was socially acceptable to leave.

"You need to get out more," Ryan had said on the walk over. "You're turning into a manila folder."

"I like manila folders," I muttered. "Orderly. Dependable."

He laughed, predictably. "Tonight's different. The Velvet Note is a vibe, man. Just wait."

I had waited. I was still waiting. And then she happened.

It wasn't so much a moment as a shift in the air.

One second, I was zoning out while some man read a poem about rain, and the next, I was on my feet. Literally. Because someone had bumped into me.

Actually, scratch that.

I had bumped into her.

Coffee sloshed, her tray jostled, and her delicate gasp, soft but sharp, cut through the mellow music playing in the background.

"Whoa—hey! Careful, Hemingway."

"Oh God. I'm so sorry," I stammered, stepping back and almost tripping over the stool behind me. "I didn't see you there."

Her eyes met mine, sharp and amused, like I was an unexpected jazz riff she hadn't planned but was intrigued by, anyway. She balanced the tray like she'd done it a thousand times, her wrist flicking in a smooth motion that kept the ceramic cups steady.

"No harm done," she said. "But this guy over here was two seconds from getting an espresso facial."

I flushed, brushing imaginary lint off my coat like it would make me feel less idiotic.

"Let me, um, help you clean that up?" I offered.

She raised a perfectly arched brow. "Are you planning on following me around with napkins all night?"

"I could be convinced," I said before I realised how that sounded. "I mean, not in a creepy way, I just meant..."

"I know what you meant," she said with a smirk that made my brain go static.

"Izzy," she added after a pause. "Well, Isabelle Laurant, technically. But no one calls me that unless I'm in trouble."

"Daniel. Carter," I said, trying not to sound like I was reading off a name tag. "And I'm probably in trouble."

She laughed. A warm, rich sound, like a saxophone solo melting into the early hours of the morning. "I'll give you a pass, Daniel Carter. First offense and all."

Just then, Ryan appeared at my elbow with that obnoxious grin that told me he'd seen the whole thing.

"I see you've met the owner of The Velvet Note and our hostess with the mostest," he said. "Izzy, this is my very grumpy best friend and reluctant literary event hostage."

Izzy winked. "Ah. The folder man."

"Manila folder, specifically," I muttered.

"Colour me intrigued."

She floated away before I could form a response, the tray balanced with elegance, her presence trailing like perfume. I sank back onto my stool, pulse still thudding like the bass line humming under the café's speakers.

"Why didn't you tell me she was the owner?" I hissed.

Ryan shrugged. "Because you would've said something self-deprecating and left early."

Fair.

Later, while pretending to admire the shelves lined with vintage records and dog-eared novels, I found myself near the counter again, drawn like a moth to a stylish flame.

Izzy was behind it now, moving like she was half dancing, half-working. She hummed under her breath as she wiped down the espresso machine. I recognised the melody; some old Sarah Vandenburg number my grandmother used to play.

"You sing," I said, blurting it before I had a plan.

She looked up, startled, then smiled slowly. "Guilty. You've got a good ear."

"Used to be sharper. My mom was a music teacher."

"And now?"

"Now I write press releases about tax software."

She winced theatrically. "Really? That is a tragic fall from grace."

"Tell me about it."

She leaned her elbow on the counter, chin in her hand. "So, what brought you here tonight, Daniel Carter? Besides the gravitational pull of my latte artistry."

I chuckled. "My best friend thinks I need 'exposure to culture.'"

"Do you?"

"Probably. I've been in a rut."

Izzy tilted her head. "Work rut? Life rut? Existential ennui?"

"All the above."

"Well," she said, straightening, "you're in the right place. Art. Music. Bad poetry. We specialise in existential awakening. And cinnamon rolls."

"Dangerous combination."

"Live a little."

She poured herself a small cup of something dark and handed me another. No charge.

"What's this?" I asked.

"House blend. Stronger than your regrets."

I took a sip.

It was bold, warm, a little sweet at the end. Like her.

"Okay," I said, setting it down. "This is the best thing I've tasted all year."

"Don't sound so surprised," she teased. "We take our brews seriously here."

I looked around.

The soft clink of cups, the low lighting, the velvet curtains, the man at the mic now talking about love like it was both a war and a lullaby.

"You built all this?" I asked.

"Piece by piece," she said. "After I stopped touring. The road was beautiful, but not kind. I wanted roots. A place where the music didn't have to chase applause."

I nodded. "It's working."

Her expression softened. "Thanks. That means more than you think."

We stood there for a beat, the air between us charged with something I hadn't felt in a long time. Not quite a spark. More like recognition. Like we'd once heard the same song in different lifetimes.

Then she said, "You know, you're not as grumpy as advertised."

"Give me time."

She laughed again.

When the event ended, the crowd thinned, and Ryan was deep in conversation with a short-haired poet who seemed to be quoting Rilke in German. I lingered by the bar, watching Izzy lock up the tip jar.

"You off the clock now?" I asked.

She glanced up. "Technically."

"Feel like talking to a reluctant tax software writer a bit longer?"

She paused, then came around the counter and leaned beside me. "Only if you promise to tell me something real."

"Like?"

"Like why you really came tonight?"

I looked at her, really looked at her, the curve of her cheek, the flicker of curiosity in her gaze. "Because some part of me hoped that something different might happen. Something I didn't plan."

"And?"

"And I bumped into someone who makes excellent coffee and makes me forget I hate poetry."

She smiled. Soft, unguarded.

"Daniel Carter," she said, "I think you just passed the vibe check."

"Is that the final exam?"

"Nope. Just the midterm."

"I'm a good crammer."

"I bet you are. I bet you are," she hummed with a speculative glint in her eye.

We talked—about music, and cities we'd both loved, and stories we never thought we'd tell anyone—until chairs were stacked and lights were dimmed.

She told me about losing her voice once, during a set in Chicago, and how silence scared her more than anything.

I told her I had written nothing real in years.

She leaned in, her voice low and velvet smooth. "Maybe you just need the right soundtrack."

"Yeah, maybe I do."

Daniel Carter

Izzy

As I closed the café and locked the front door, I poured myself a glass of wine before sitting down on the bar.

Daniel Carter was on my mind.

He had the kind of quiet presence that didn't immediately grab your attention, but once you noticed him, you couldn't quite look away. Daniel had looked to be in his fifties, though there was a certain timelessness about his features. His hair—the colour of salt and pepper, with the salt perhaps just beginning to win out—was neatly combed but held a hint of a wave that suggested he wasn't overly fussy. It framed a face that, while showing the lines of a life lived—especially around his thoughtful brown eyes¬—held a surprisingly youthful quality when he smiled.

He wasn't a big man, but there was a sturdy build to him, a comfortable weight that spoke of long hours spent perhaps more with books than barbells. His hands, when he gestured slightly as he spoke about some obscure poet, were surprisingly elegant, the fingers long and slender. He was dressed simply in a well-worn tweed jacket over a blue button-down shirt, the kind of attire that felt both professorial and utterly unpretentious. There was a small, almost imperceptible ink stain on his index finger. It was a detail I found strangely endearing. It hinted at the world he inhabited; a tangible connection to the words he clearly loved.

It wasn't his physical appearance alone that held my interest, though there was a gentle attractiveness to him. It was the way his eyes crinkled at the corners when he spoke with genuine enthusiasm, the slight furrow in his brow when he considered a point, and the overall air of quiet intelligence that seemed to radiate from him. There was a vulnerability there too, I sensed, a subtle shadow that perhaps a recent divorce might have cast (though I never asked), but it only added to the intrigue.

He wasn't trying to impress, and that, I realised, was perhaps the most captivating thing about him.

Downing the last of the wine, I gathered my purse and headed to the back, where my car was parked. As I locked The Velvet Note up, I wondered if Daniel Carter would come back for another coffee.

3

Isabelle 'Izzy' Laurant

Daniel

Ryan and I left the Velvet Note.

Ryan was still agitated by his last conversation, and I, well, I was totally immersed in Isabelle 'Izzy' Laurant.

Izzy.

The name itself had a certain vibrancy, and it suited her perfectly.

She'd looked about my age, maybe just a sight year or two younger, but she carried herself with the energy of someone a decade younger. Her eyes, a striking shade of emerald that seemed to sparkle with amusement and a hint of mischief, were the first thing you noticed. A cascade of silver-streaked dark curls framed them, even as they looked like they had a life of their own framed them, escaping the loose knot she'd attempted at the nape of her neck.

She wasn't conventionally beautiful in a delicate way, but there was a captivating warmth and strength in her features.

Her smile was wide and genuine, crinkling the corners of her eyes and revealing a hint of a gap between her front teeth that somehow only added to her charm. You could imagine that smile lighting up a smoky jazz club stage.

Her hands, the kind that looked like they'd seen some action, were adorned with a few chunky silver rings. She'd wore a vibrant, flowing dress in shades of deep blues and greens, paired with comfortable-looking leather sandals. There was a smudge of flour on her cheek, which she brushed away with a laugh when she noticed me looking. It spoke of someone who wasn't afraid to get her hands dirty, someone who was truly present in her own world.

There was a certain earthiness about her, an unapologetic confidence that was incredibly alluring. She moved with a natural grace, even as she bustled behind the counter, and her voice, still carrying the rich, slightly husky timbre I imagined had once filled the jazz halls, was both warm and commanding. She had a way of making you feel instantly at ease, like you'd known her for years, and yet there was a depth in her gaze that hinted at stories untold, experiences that had shaped her into this fascinating woman. She wasn't just a café owner; well, she did make one hell of a coffee. I could sense a whole life lived behind those bright green eyes, and I wanted to know every single detail.

"I am guessing you enjoyed the night out," said Ryan, interrupting my thoughts.

"Yes, I did," and I left it at that.

4

The Invitation

Daniel

It had been a week since I'd last seen Izzy.

Seven days of playing the whole evening back like a song stuck on a loop.

Her laugh, the smell of roasted espresso, the moment our conversation shifted from surface chatter to something… else.

I'd told myself it didn't mean anything.

People flirted all the time, coffee got poured; places like The Velvet Note were designed to feel cinematic. That was the trick.

But even as I sat in my apartment, trying to focus on work—on a marketing proposal for an enterprise invoicing platform (exciting, I know)—I stared out the window, thinking of her. Of how warm her eyes were when she talked about music. Of how I had felt something loosen in me, just a little, when I told her I had written nothing real in years. And she didn't look away.

Still, I was torn.

Since the divorce, I'd convinced myself I wasn't relationship material.

Sandra had said as much when she packed her boxes.

"You build walls and then complain no one gets in," she'd said, folding jumpers with surgical precision. "I tried. But you make everything harder than it needs to be, Daniel."

She wasn't wrong.

I over-thought; I second-guessed. I got scared when things got good.

Maybe I was the common denominator. The man who couldn't make it work, even when it mattered.

But maybe, I thought as I pulled on a jacket, I can just get a coffee. Nothing loaded. Just caffeine and ambience.

If she wasn't there, fine.

If she was… well, I'd figure it out.

The Velvet Note was quieter than I remembered.

Midweek, after the dinner rush; a few regulars chatted near the window, and a soft piano drifted through the speakers. It wasn't live tonight, but the mood still felt rich, like pages turning slowly in a worn book.

I took a seat near the back, where the lighting dipped just enough to feel intimate without being shadowy. A server I didn't recognise came over with a notepad and a smile.

"House blend?" she asked.

"Sure. That'd be great."

I took out my phone and was halfway through checking my email out of habit, not necessity, when I felt someone approach the table. I looked up, and there she was.

Izzy.

Hair in a loose bun this time, apron slung casually over a navy jumpsuit, sleeves rolled to the elbow. She looked like someone who belonged in an oil painting and didn't care.

"Well, well," she said, crossing her arms. "Mr Manila Folder returns."

I smiled, couldn't help it. "Trying to branch out. Maybe add a splash of colour."

"Chartreuse, perhaps?"

"Let's not get ahead of ourselves."

She slid into the chair opposite mine without asking. "I was wondering if you'd come back."

"I almost didn't."

"Why not?"

"Because…" then stopped. "Because I overthink everything."

"Sounds exhausting."

"It is."

She tilted her head, studying me like she was reading between lines. "But you came anyway."

"Because your coffee is the best I've had all year," I said.

"Mmm." She nodded. "Right. The coffee."

I cleared my throat, suddenly warm. "Okay, maybe the company helped."

"Good save."

The server dropped off two coffees with a soft clink and a smile at Izzy, then disappeared behind the bar.

Izzy's fingers curled around her own mug. "You look better this week," she said. "Less tightly wound."

I stuck out my left leg and rolled up a jean pant leg and pointed. "See, I even wore runners instead of loafers. It's progress."

She laughed again, easily, like we were picking up from last time, not navigating whatever this was.

"So," she said after a beat. "I was thinking I've got to close up in a couple of hours. Would you want to stick around? Have a nightcap? Just a quiet drink after hours."

I blinked. "Like, here?"

"Yeah. I usually do a wind-down drink before heading home. Sometimes it's bourbon. Sometimes just chamomile tea and bad jazz. Other times wine. But I'd like the company tonight."

She said it so simply. No weight. No pressure.

Still, I hesitated. Because some ancient part of me still thought saying yes to people meant risking disappointment. Or worse, causing it.

But then I looked at her, at the openness in her face, the calm certainty that reminded me not everything had to be tangled.

"Okay," I said. "I'll stay."

Her smile was small but genuine. "Good."

The lights dimmed even further when the last customer left. Izzy locked the front door, flipped the sign, then moved around the café with practiced ease, humming something I didn't recognise.

"You always sing under your breath?" I asked.

"Always," she said. "It's like a second heartbeat."

She emerged from the back with two glasses and a bottle of something amber.

"I vote bourbon tonight," she said, setting them down at the bar. "But if you're feeling tea and existential dread, I won't judge."

"Bourbon's perfect."

We clinked glasses, and for a while, we just sat in the quiet.

No expectations. No rush.

Eventually, she spoke. "So, Daniel Carter. What's your story?"

I took a sip. "Divorced. Mildly neurotic. Works in corporate PR but secretly wants to write something that makes someone feel something."

"That's a solid headline."

"And you?"

"Ex-jazz singer. Burned out on hotel lounges and record label promises. Built a sanctuary out of caffeine and velvet. Still miss the stage sometimes."

I turned to her. "Why'd you stop singing?"

She looked down at her glass. "I didn't stop. I paused. Big difference."

I nodded. "Fair."

There was a long pause; comfortable, not awkward.

Then she said, "You know, you don't have to prove anything to be here."

I blinked at her. "What do you mean?"

"You keep waiting for the other shoe to drop. I see it: the second-guessing, the overthinking. But maybe this is just, you know, nice. Maybe that's enough."

I looked at her then, really looked, and for the first time in a long time, I didn't feel like I had to apologise for being a little broken.

"Thank you," I said quietly.

"For the bourbon?"

"For letting me stay."

She gave me a soft smile, and we sat there, two people with pasts, trying to figure out if maybe the future didn't have to be so scary.

Outside, the city moved on. Inside, time slowed down.

And in that small, velvet-coloured pocket of the night, I didn't feel torn anymore.

I felt… curious.

Hopeful, even.

5

Dim Lights

Daniel

We lost track of time.

One glass turned into two, then three, then four, and then I lost count. At some point, Izzy dug up an old record from behind the bar. A soft, crackling Billie Holiday number that made the mood even smoother around the café. The lights were dim, her shoes were off, and we were slouched in mismatched armchairs near the window, a bottle of bourbon between us and the city asleep beyond the glass with just a few cars passing by.

I didn't know why we talked like people who didn't expect to see the other again. It was the kind of honesty you could only share with someone you trusted, or someone you thought might vanish with the sunrise.

She told me about a man named Javier—her first genuine love.

"We were both twenty-one," she said, staring into the middle distance. "He was Cuban and played the trumpet like he was chasing God. We lived out of a van for two summers, touring small venues and dive bars. He smelled like cedarwood and bourbon, and he used to leave notes in my shoes. Literal paper notes. Little poems. Silly things."

"What happened?"

"He didn't want stillness," she said. "And I did. Eventually. I craved something that didn't disappear after every encore."

Then there was Michael, a sharp-tongued, jazz loving producer Izzy had met in New Orleans. They'd had fire. Passion. "But too much fire burns the house down," she said with a shrug. "He was brilliant, though. He pushed me. I still think about him when I'm writing set lists."

She stopped and took a sip of her drink and continued.

"There was Max. He wanted to marry me. Move to the suburbs. Two-car garage, get a dog and named it Barkley. He had it all planned out." She paused. "But I couldn't breathe in the life he wanted. I said no. He never forgave me."

"Do you regret it?" I asked.

She considered. "Sometimes. On quiet mornings when it rains and I look out a window. But I think if I'd said yes, I wouldn't be here right now. Talking to you."

I let that settle between us.

She sipped slowly from her glass, eyes scanning mine. "Your turn."

I exhaled. "Sandra."

She nodded, patient.

"We were good once," I said. "Met at a literary festival in Vermont. She asked if I wanted to get a drink, and I thought she was the bravest person I'd ever met. She made me feel seen. For a long time, that was enough."

"What changed?"

"I think I stopped letting her in. Work got demanding. I got quiet. Thoughtful in the worst way. I was always waiting for things to settle before being present. But life never really settles, does it?"

Izzy's eyes softened. "No. It doesn't."

"I kept thinking I'd write a book. I kept saying, 'After this campaign, after this quarter, after the next deadline.' She wanted a partner. I was too busy trying to be a project manager for my heart."

There was no bitterness when I said it. Just truth and a low hum of sadness.

"She left at the end of spring two years ago," I added. "We said it was mutual. It wasn't. She was just the one brave enough to walk."

Izzy reached across and laid her hand gently over mine. "I'm sorry."

I didn't pull away.

"Do you miss her?"

"I miss the version of me when I was with her," I admitted. "I felt more… hopeful."

She smiled, bittersweet. "That version isn't gone, Daniel. Just sleeping."

"Maybe."

We sat with that. The hours crept on. The bottle dipped lower and our voices grew softer.

We talked about dreams, hers of opening a second Velvet Note in the French Quarter in New Orleans. Mine of finally finishing that novel I started seven years ago about a failed jazz pianist who hides inside a bookstore.

"I like that," she said. "There's music in it already."

There was music in this night, too.

And then something happened, something small and seismic. She reached up to tuck a loose curl behind her ear, and the movement, so delicate, so unconscious, struck me like a match to dry paper. I lit up!

Her bare shoulder caught the light. Her eyes met mine with a kind of open question in them.

And I felt it.

A shift.

Something stirring in me I thought had long since rusted over. A pulse of want—not lust, not nostalgia. Hope.

The real, reckless kind that creeps in uninvited and sits in the empty chair beside you.

She said nothing. Just looked at me for a beat longer than polite conversation would allow. And I wondered, Where is this going?

What were we doing, two people in our fifties, bruised but breathing, drinking away the hours like 20 somethings chasing possibility?

And why, for the first time in years, did it feel okay to not know the answer?

I leaned back, laughing at something she'd said a moment ago. I couldn't even remember the line, just that it was dry and unexpected and so very Izzy.

My stomach ached from it.

My cheeks were warm. I was laughing. Actually laughing. And I realised it had been years since I'd done that without forcing it.

"Goodness," I said, wiping my eyes. "You're dangerous."

She smiled. "Only to men who think they're immune to joy."

"You know, I used to think I was."

"Not anymore?"

I looked at her.

The way she curled her legs up beneath her.

The way she tilted her head when I spoke.

The way she didn't seem afraid of silence.

"No," I said. "Not anymore."

Outside, the sky was shifting. Dark blue bleeding toward silver. Early light crept in through the window like little rays, brushing over tabletops and half-drunk glasses.

"I should probably get going," I said, though I didn't move.

Izzy's smile was tired but warm. "You could stay until the sun's up."

"The sun is coming up and it wouldn't be the worst idea I've ever had."

"No," she said, her voice barely above a whisper. "It wouldn't."

Something was happening.

Something unplanned, unspoken.

And I wasn't running from it.

Not today.

6

New Thoughts

Daniel

The streets were hushed when I stepped out of The Velvet Note.

Dawn hadn't fully broken, but it was coming. The new day was arriving, the way it always did, whether or not I was ready.

The door clicked shut behind me; I turned and the last thing I saw was her smile as she closed the blinds on the door.

For a second, I stood still on the sidewalk, the cool morning air brushing against my flushed skin. I could still feel the warmth of her hand on mine. Still hear the softness of her laugh in the spaces between cars passing in the distance.

I should have felt tired. The bourbon, the late hour. God, I hadn't stayed up this late in ages. It should've dragged me straight under like an anchor. But it didn't. My body was buzzing, electric with memory. My mind wouldn't stop.

What the hell had just happened?

I hailed a cab because my legs didn't trust me. The driver said little, just nodded when I gave him my address. I leaned against the window and watched the city streets slide by; quiet now but getting ready for the influx of daily labourers coming in to work. For some reason, I thought the world felt different than it had the night before.

Brighter. Less heavy.

Or maybe I was different.

Izzy.

Her name echoed like a bell in my chest.

When I got home, I dropped my keys into the bowl by the door and kicked off my shoes instead of placing them on my hall bench. My unit felt colder than I remembered. Why had I never noticed all the muted greys and clean surfaces? Why was everything so neat? Way too neat. A little too curated, like I'd been trying to live in a catalogue of "respectable healing post-divorce" instead of an actual home.

I wandered into the kitchen, poured a glass of water I didn't drink, then stood there holding it, staring at nothing in particular. The clock read 6:12 a.m.

I took out my mobile, dialled the office line, and waited for the beep.

"Hey, it's Daniel," I said, rubbing my forehead. "I'm not great today. Something's off. I'm going to take a sick day. Nothing serious, I just need to rest. Thanks."

I ended the call and shuffled into the bedroom. I peeled off my jacket and flopped onto the bed face-first. My limbs felt heavy. My eyes stung. I didn't even bother pulling the covers over me.

I closed my eyes.

The liquor should've knocked me out cold.

Usually, it did. But not tonight—or was it this morning?

Because all I could think about was her.

Izzy.

The sound of her voice: velvety, a little husky from too much talking. The way her lips curled when she said something honest, something a little vulnerable. The way her eyes didn't flinch when I told her the truth about Sandra.

Why did it feel like I knew her already?

It was dangerous, wasn't it?

Feeling this way.

Hopeful.

Curious.

Open.

All the things I'd buried after the divorce, after the months of therapy and careful detachment. After I told myself that what Sandra and I had was some singular, once in a lifetime story, and that since I'd failed at it, there was no point in trying again.

But Izzy had unravelled something in me.

Not because she was beautiful—though God, she was—or because she flirted or poured me bourbon or told stories that made me laugh harder than I have in years. It was the way she listened. Like every sentence I spoke was the first line of a song she wanted to learn by heart.

I'd forgotten what it was like to be seen like that.

And that scared the hell out of me.

The living shitty hell.

Am I ready?

That was the question chasing itself around my skull.

Had I learned enough from what fell apart with Sandra to not repeat the same dance with someone new?

I knew my faults.

My silences. My tendency to retreat into work or logic when things got too raw.

I knew how I let the moment pass, waiting for the "right time" that never came. Could I be better now?

Could I choose to be present, even when it was messy and uncertain?

I didn't know. But for the first time in a long time, I wanted to try.

And that in itself was so much more terrifying in its own way.

Because wanting something again meant I could lose it. And loss, after hope, always cut deeper.

Still, as I laid there with my heart doing somersaults and my thoughts running in overlapping circles, I couldn't help but feel alive. Stretched in some quiet, tender way. Like I'd been holding my breath for months and someone finally told me I could exhale.

The sky outside my window was shifting; soft grey gently yielding to the bright embrace of gold.

And finally, slowly, my mind drifted.

My last thought before sleep was not a question.

It wasn't fear, doubt, or regret.

It was her.

Izzy.

The way she looked at me when she said, "You don't have to prove anything to be here."

Maybe that was true.

7

A Reluctant Goodbye

Izzy

I stood at the front door long after Daniel had gone.

The soft click of the latch echoed a little louder than I expected in the hush of the empty café. I reached up and ran the blinds down with a practiced tug, but I didn't move after that. My hand lingered on the cord. My eyes stayed fixed on the spot where he'd been, just moments ago, his silhouette lit by the soft blue promise of dawn.

What the hell just happened?

I should've been wiping down counters or counting the till like I always did. I should've been humming some half-remembered melody to keep me company while the quiet pressed in. But I didn't move.

Instead, I stood there like someone waiting for the next act in a play she hadn't realised she'd been cast in giving him a reluctant goodbye.

Daniel Carter.

The name itself didn't sound dangerous.

Not like Javier or Max or any of the other beautiful, reckless men who had come and gone from my life, like firestorms. And yet, there was something about him. Something still. Something steady and slow burning. Like he didn't have to rush to the centre of the stage, he'd just get there when it was time.

That scared me more than any trumpet player or tightly wound producer ever had.

I'd been through a litany of men, hadn't I?

Men who dazzled, men who devoured, men who needed to be saved or who wanted to save me.

Each one with his own rhythm, his own story.

And every time I'd let them in. Even for a season, it always ended with me alone, a little older, a little wiser, a little more certain that maybe I was better off solo.

But Daniel.

He wasn't loud. He wasn't trying to impress me.

He listened.

He asked questions and actually waited for the answers. He looked at me like he was paying attention, and that…well, that was more intoxicating than any sweet talk.

My fingertips still tingled from where they'd brushed his hand. From where our eyes locked when we talked about things, most people kept hidden behind neat smiles and pleasant shrugs.

He said I was dangerous. Ha.

Maybe it was him I should be worried about.

Because I didn't let people see me anymore.

Not really.

Not like that.

And yet tonight, I had.

I'd wanted to.

The clock above the bar chimed softly. Six o'clock.

The early sun poured like gold streaks across the floorboards, and just like that, the spell broke. Reality trickled back in, cool and unwelcome.

I blinked. Enough, Izzy.

I grabbed my purse from under the counter and double-checked the locks, muscle memory carrying me through the motions.

Out the back door.

Into the car.

Keys in the ignition.

Radio off.

I drove the familiar streets in silence.

The city looked like it was holding its breath neither night nor morning, just the in-between.

Just like me.

When I pulled into the driveway, I sat for a few extra minutes in the car, engine off. The warmth of the sunrise creeped through the windshield. I could've walked in. I should've. But I didn't.

Because the moment I crossed the threshold, I knew his name would follow me inside. Like perfume on a borrowed jacket. Faint, but impossible to ignore.

Daniel.

Damn him.

I kicked off my shoes in the hallway and dropped my purse on the bench. Walked into the lounge and sank into the sofa like it had been calling me home. I didn't turn on the lights. The soft early morning glow was enough.

I curled one leg under me, my blanket already waiting in its usual corner. But I didn't reach for it yet.

My mind was still racing.

What is happening to me?

He made me laugh.

God, really laugh.

Not that polite café chuckle I handed out with oat milk lattes and witty banter. The kind of laugh that came from the gut, unfiltered and real.

He looked at me like he didn't just want to sleep with me—though I saw it in his eyes, the spark, the question—but like he wanted to know me. The person under the songs and the smiles and the coffee-stained apron.

That was new. And terrifying.

I'd built this little world of mine carefully.

The Velvet Note wasn't just a café; it was my fortress. My confession booth. My stage.

I made the rules there.

I set the tone.

I decided who got close.

And yet I invited him to stay.

I asked him to stay.

Damn him.

Was I really ready to open that door again?

Was I going to take another leap?

And then a softer voice in my mind whispered, Why not?

What if this time it wasn't about fire or flight, about trying to fit someone else's rhythm into my melody? What if this time it was just a duet? No performances. No apologies.

Just two people who'd been broken before and were maybe ready to make something whole.

Daniel Carter, you are a damn sweet, unexpected thing. I tipped my head back against the couch. You might just be dangerous after all.

I finally pulled the blanket over my shoulders, tucked my knees to my chest. The sky was brighter now, blushing pink at the edges.

Sleep tugged at me gently, no longer willing to be ignored.

I let my eyes fall closed, and just before the world faded…

His name.

Not spoken aloud.

Not dreamed.

Just felt.

Daniel.

8

A Slow Dance

Daniel

I told myself I wasn't going back.

I even made it through the day of waiting just to end up standing outside The Velvet Note again. My heart thumped like I was about to walk into some kind of confessional.

It was just before closing; later than anyone would normally show up for a caffeine fix or listen to the last jazz gig. The last few patrons were filtering out, the sound of their goodbyes muffled through the glass. I waited until the final one had left before I pushed the door open. The bell above the door chimed, low and warm.

I stepped inside, locking it behind me.

She was behind the counter, wiping it down with a dish towel, hair piled lazily on top of her head. When she looked up and saw me, there wasn't even a flicker of surprise. Just that slow, confident smile that had already etched itself into the back of my mind.

"I thought you might come—well, I hoped you would. I told Emily to go home early," she said, her voice dipped in velvet and dusk.

I shrugged, suddenly feeling like a teenager with his hands in his pockets. "I, uh… couldn't sleep."

"That makes two of us." She tossed the towel aside and gestured toward one of the stools. "You want coffee?"

I hesitated. "Not tonight."

Her smile shifted slightly, something quieter underneath. "Wine, then."

"I won't say no."

She disappeared into the back, returned a moment later with a dusty bottle of red and two glasses that didn't match. Of course they didn't. This place wasn't about matching; this place was about stories.

She poured without ceremony, handed me a glass, and raised hers in an almost-toast. "To sleepless nights," she said.

"And strange company," I added.

We both sipped.

I don't know what made her do it. Maybe it was the wine, or the hour, or something in the air, but without saying a word, she crossed over to the small record player she kept in the corner, near the stage. The thing looked ancient, but she treated it like a treasure. With careful fingers, she selected a vinyl from a thin stack, blew dust from the sleeve, and placed the needle down.

A low crackle filled the room. Then a trumpet, smooth and sultry. Peter Shales, of course; a jazz singer known for his performances of the Great American Songbook and Broadway standards. A glorious voice; easy for dancing.

She turned to look at me, one eyebrow raised. "Do you dance, Daniel?"

"Not well."

"Perfect," she said, and held out her hand.

Something in me unclenched.

I set the wine down, stepped toward her, and took her hand. It was small and warm in mine, calloused at the edges from years of cups, keys, and life. She slid the other hand to my shoulder. I rested mine at the small of her back.

And just like that, we were dancing.

Well, something like it.

We moved slow, off-beat, unsure of who was leading and who was following. Our feet bumped. She laughed—God, that laugh—and I couldn't help but join her.

"I told you," I said. "Not well."

"You're doing fine," she said, her voice low now as her cheek brushed mine.

The café was empty around us. We paused to stack the chairs on tables and then continued dancing. The city outside had gone quiet again. Well, it seemed so to me. I didn't know nor care. It was just us, swaying in a room that felt suddenly too intimate and tender for words.

"You know," she said softly, "this wasn't what I expected."

"Tonight?"

"You."

I leaned back just enough to see her face. "That makes two of us."

She looked at me for a long beat, like she was trying to read a lyric she hadn't heard before.

"I've had a lot of men look at me," she said finally. "But it's been a long time since someone really saw me."

"Izzy…"

"You don't have to say anything," she said, resting her head lightly against my chest. "Let's just dance."

So, we did.

We danced through the end of the song, and the one after that. We laughed when we nearly tripped over a power cord.

I twirled her once, badly, and she bumped the table, nearly spilled the wine glasses.

It was ridiculous.

It was real.

I didn't know where this was going. I didn't know if I was ready.

But standing there, with her heartbeat close to mine and her smile pressed into my shoulder, I felt something I hadn't in a long, long time.

Hope.

And I wasn't about to let it slip away.

Not with her.

Still, I had responsibilities. Work. A looming conference in Melbourne in two days. My flight was early, and my presentation was earlier.

As I slipped on my coat, Izzy tilted her head in that way she did, like she could read me before I even spoke.

"I have to head out," I said, reluctantly.

"Oh?" she asked, though I think she already knew.

"I've got a conference in Melbourne. I'm flying out in two days. Have to prep tomorrow, meetings, slides, all the usual chaos."

She leaned back against the counter, arms folded but eyes soft. "How long will you be gone?"

"Five days. Maybe six if the post-event networking gets heavy."

Her lips curved. "Fancy way to say you'll be drinking with nerds."

"Accurate," I chuckled. "But I'll come back here. First night back, if you're around."

She stepped forward, touched my arm gently. "I'll be here."

9

Denial Is a River in Egypt

Daniel

That touch stayed with me the entire flight to Melbourne. Through every speech, every boring networking dinner, every polite nod. I kept thinking about her. Her voice, that easy laugh, the way her eyes seemed to look right through my armour. I even caught myself humming one of the jazz records she played when I was alone in the hotel.

When I finally landed back in the city, tired and jet lagged but oddly lighter, there was no question where I'd go first after dropping my stuff at home and freshening up.

The Velvet Note.

It was early evening, just before the usual rush. The sun hung low through the windows, casting amber across the café floor. A few tables were occupied, quiet chatter threading through the air.

And there she was, Izzy.

Laughing at something, her hand resting gently on the shoulder of a younger man seated at the corner of the bar. He leaned in slightly, smiling in a way that made something in my chest twist.

They were close.

Too close.

Something sank in me.

A ridiculous, unearned sense of betrayal bloomed fast and hot.

Was it jealousy? Insecurity?

Probably both.

Either way, it rose like a nasty taste in my throat.

I should've just walked out. Should've left it alone. But I didn't.

I stepped forward, still trying to carry some veneer of calm, and Izzy spotted me. Her face lit up—genuine, warm. "Daniel! You're back."

I forced a smile. "Just got in a few hours ago. Thought I'd drop by."

She turned to the man beside her. "Daniel, this is Freddy."

Freddy stood and extended his hand easily, like he'd been expecting me.

"Nice to meet you," he said, his voice smooth, open. "Heard your name once or twice."

I shook his hand, though the knot in my stomach hadn't eased.

God, I hate him, I thought.

He gestured for me to take the seat beside him. I hesitated, then sat.

The three of us chatted casually. Had a coffee, spoke a bit of travel, there was even a bit of jazz trivia thrown in. Freddy was smart. Charming. And undeniably young—younger than me, for sure, by at least ten years.

I watched the way he looked at Izzy. Comfortable. Familiar.

And something inside me cracked. I couldn't help it.

I leaned forward, trying to sound casual and failing utterly. "So, Freddy, what are your intentions with Izzy?"

The moment the words left my mouth, I regretted them.

Izzy blinked. Freddy looked at me like I'd just asked him if he believed in unicorns.

"My intentions?" he repeated, then let out a sharp laugh. "With Izzy?"

He looked at her, incredulous.

"I'm Izzy's younger brother," he said, clearly amused. "What possible intentions could I have outside of bugging her, stealing her last cookies, and getting free coffee?"

The silence that followed was painful.

Then Izzy burst out laughing.

"Oh my God, Daniel," she wheezed. "You thought—?"

"I—" I rubbed the back of my neck. "Okay, I'm a dummkopf."

Freddy raised a brow. "A what?"

"It's… German. For an idiot."

He grinned. "I like it."

I glanced at him, and to my surprise, added, "I think I like you too."

Freddy clinked his coffee mug against mine. "You're alright, man. Just protective. I dig it."

Izzy, still chuckling, shook her head. "You two are going to be trouble. I can feel it."

But I felt something else now.

Relief. Clarity. A little humility, sure, but even that felt good.

It meant I cared.

Just as I was relaxing again, basking in the warm glow of not being a total idiot, the door to The Velvet Note opened and in came a familiar whirlwind in a leather jacket and worn boots.

Ryan.

Of course. I should've known.

He scanned the café, eyes landing on me instantly. A wide, smug grin spread across his face like he'd just won a bet.

"I knew you'd be here," he called, loud enough to make Izzy raise an amused eyebrow.

Freddy leaned back in his chair, watching the newcomer with interest. Ryan strode over with his usual flair, clapping me hard on the back like he was trying to wake my spine up.

"Melbourne couldn't keep you away long, huh?" he said with a wink. "Jet lagged and already sniffing around the jazz café. Figures."

Freddy chuckled. "You must be Ryan."

"Guilty," he said, offering his hand. "And you must be the infamous Freddy. I've heard… frankly, way too little. Izzy likes to keep things close to the chest."

"I prefer 'mysterious,'" he muttered.

Freddy leaned forward, grinning. "So you two have known each other for a while?"

Ryan pulled a chair over without asking and dropped into it with the casual entitlement of someone who's made himself comfortable in every room his whole life.

"Since university," he said. "Roommates. I once saved him from a questionable tuna sandwich and a disastrous poetry reading on the same night."

"Neither of those things are true," I said flatly.

"Debatable." He turned to Izzy, undeterred. "So, tell me, how are you putting up with him?"

Izzy grinned. "With patience. And wine."

Ryan gave a dramatic nod. "Wise woman."

Despite the eye rolls and the mortifying memories he was clearly lining up in his mental slingshot, I was glad he was here. Ryan had a way of crashing into things but also anchoring them. He could cut tension with a joke, make anyone feel like they'd known him for years.

But of course, he also had zero filter.

"So," Ryan said, looking between me and Izzy, "are we officially in the flirty café romance stage, or are we still pretending this is all caffeine?"

I groaned. "Ryan…"

Izzy didn't miss a beat. "I don't know. What's the stage right before that?"

"Lingering glances over espresso? 'Accidental slow dancing'?" Freddy offered, clearly enjoying this too much.

"I hate all of you," I muttered into my coffee.

Ryan smirked. "See? Daniel gets all prickly when he's falling for someone. Am I correct, Daniel?"

Izzy met my eyes, and something passed between us. Not a look of embarrassment or denial, just…

"Noted," she said softly.

Ryan turned to Freddy, clearly on a roll. "So, how are you handling the new individual in this picture, Freddy? Does he pass inspection?"

"He is OK by my book, but then again, I am not seeing him, right, sis?"

Ryan blinked. "Oh. Well damn, Izzy, I was about to warn you about dating older men."

We all laughed, even me, though I shook my head and gave Ryan the most unimpressed look I could muster.

He continued with a grin. "Did you know, Freddy, that Daniel can be the jealous type?"

"No kidding. I would have never guessed it."

"Indeed, he can be. He'll deny it." He shrugged comically before grinning at the other man. "By the way, Freddy, did you know that denial is a river in Egypt?"

Freddy almost choked on that last one, but Ryan wasn't about to stop. I dropped my head into my hands and groaned as he continued. Finally, after what seemed like forever, he paused to take a breath and Freddy broke in.

"Ryan, you come here more often that I do. Have they started holding hands yet?" asked Freddy.

I groaned. "Will you stop?" I almost screamed.

They both just sipped their coffees, all smug.

But underneath the jokes and the easy banter, I felt something settle. These three had started an orbit around me in a way that didn't feel temporary.

It felt like the beginning of something.

And when Izzy looked at me, her eyes soft and sparkling, I knew she felt it too.

Whatever this was—we were in it now.

And to paraphrase Betty Davis in the movie 'All About Eve,' fasten your seatbelts. We were in for a bumpy ride!

10

The First Kiss

Daniel

After that night at The Velvet Note, between Freddy's surprise twist, Ryan's usual chaos, and the charged glance Izzy, and I had shared, I knew I needed time with her. Real time.

Not in the buzz of her café, not over the counter with customers around, and definitely not with Ryan throwing around commentary like we were in a 90s rom com.

I wanted us uninterrupted.

No jazz playing in the background, no cups clinking, no well-meaning friends trying to decode whatever this was turning into.

So, the next day, I called her.

"Izzy," I said, a little nervous, though I wasn't sure why. "Any chance you can get away for a night? Just dinner. Just us."

There was a pause on the other end, soft static, like the world briefly held its breath.

"Depends," she said playfully. "Are you cooking?"

I laughed. "Not unless you want to experience something dangerously under-seasoned."

"I'm intrigued but also value my life. Where?"

"How do you feel about seafood by the beach?" I asked. "There's this spot I like in Manly: the Abalone Room. Great fish. Even better wine. It's quiet."

She didn't hesitate. "I'm in."

We agreed on 7 p.m. the next night.

The Abalone Room was tucked away off the main drag; dim lighting, soft jazz humming low in the background and windows looking out over the water. A minor storm had swept through earlier that day, leaving behind crisp air and the smell of salt.

When I arrived, Izzy was already there, seated at a corner table with the candlelight flickering across her features. She looked up and smiled when she saw me; something gentle and easy in it that knocked the wind out of me.

"You're early," she said.

"So are you."

We both laughed.

The waiter came, and we ordered a grilled snapper for her, blue-eyed cod for me, and a bottle of crisp white to share.

Conversation flowed without effort. We shared more stories from her days on the road, singing in dim bars and hotel lounges. How she once got caught in a monsoon in Kuala Lumpur and ended up performing for stranded tourists in a hotel lobby with a band she'd just met that morning.

"You have a way of collecting adventures," I said.

"I don't collect them," she replied, swirling her wine. "They find me."

We talked about Melbourne, about my conference, and without meaning to, I told her more about Sandra than I expected. Not out of bitterness. Just honesty. It felt safe here.

"I think," I said, "I didn't really know how to show up in that marriage. Not the way Sandra needed. I spent years avoiding conflict and mistaking that for peace."

Izzy didn't interrupt, just listened. That alone made me want to tell her more. "And now?"

"Now I want to be more awake. I don't want to sleepwalk through anything again."

She reached across the table, laid her hand over mine for a moment, her touch light but grounding.

We argued about the bill, of course. She insisted on splitting, then insisted on paying. I overruled her in the end.

"Next one's on me," she said, mock stern.

"I'll let you believe that." I replied, smiling.

Outside, the air had cooled even more. The moon hung over the bay, casting silver ripples across the water. We wandered along the boardwalk, the sea lapping gently beside us. I took our first selfie.

Izzy shivered, almost imperceptibly.

Without thinking, I shrugged off my coat and draped it around her shoulders.

She looked up at me, eyes wide, soft. The breeze caught a strand of her hair and sent it fluttering across her face.

I reached out, gently tucking it behind her ear. She leaned slightly into my touch. And before either of us could really think or hesitate, we kissed.

It wasn't dramatic or hungry. It was quiet, unsure at first, but there was a charge in it, an unexpected electricity that pulsed through my chest like a spark hitting dry wood.

When we pulled apart, I looked at her and said the first honest thing that came to mind. "Izzy, I think we both need time. Not to run away from this, but just to be sure. I don't want to leap too fast, not with something that feels this good, this real."

She didn't answer right away. Just stared at me for a long beat, her eyes searching mine like she was trying to read the spaces between my words.

Then she gave the faintest nod.

"I'm not sure I agree," she said, "but I understand."

I offered a sheepish smile. "You're dangerous, you know that?"

She smirked. "Maybe it's you who's dangerous."

We walked a little longer in silence. It was the kind of silence that felt full rather than empty.

Later, after I dropped her off at her car and watched her disappear into the street, I walked to my car and sat there and just breathed for a while.

Because something was changing.

And for the first time in a long time, I wasn't afraid of what came next.

11

The Past Comes Knocking

Daniel

The days had blurred into each other again. Emails, reports, client calls, and late nights at the office where the windows turned black before I even noticed the sun had set. I hadn't been to The Velvet Note in over three weeks, though I called Izzy whenever I could.

She never complained.

Instead, she picked up the phone with that warm, amused tone, as if she already knew my voice before I even said a word.

"Hey, stranger," she'd tease.

And I'd answer with some lame apology about meetings running late or reports piling up. But the truth was simpler: something quiet and shining had entered my life, and I feared not knowing how to handle it.

But I also knew this: I was happy. Maybe for the first time in years.

So, when my phone rang late one Wednesday afternoon, and her name flashed on the screen—Sandra, my ex—I nearly dropped it.

I stared at the name for a second, my thumb hovering over Decline. But something in me pressed Answer instead.

"Daniel," she said, her voice smaller than I remembered. "I was wondering if you could come by. Just for a bit."

I didn't ask why. Didn't push. I just said yes, and I had no idea why.

~~~

The house looked the same, but I didn't feel the same walking up to it. I knocked.

The door opened to Miriam, Sandra's oldest friend, the one who never particularly liked me, though she'd never said it aloud. Her eyes, usually sharp and quick to judge, were now dull and red-rimmed. She stepped aside silently.

That's when I knew.

Sandra was in the living room, sitting beneath a blanket that looked too heavy for spring. Her body seemed smaller, like it had folded in on itself.

She smiled when she saw me softly, like it took all the strength she had.

"Hi," she said.
~~~

"Hi," I said back, unsure if I should sit, stand, or turn and run.

"I figured it was time," she murmured, patting the couch next to her. "To tell you. Everything."

I sat. And listened.

She had uterine sarcoma.

A rare, aggressive one. Untreatable at this stage. A few weeks, maybe.

"I didn't want you to find out from anyone else," she said. "Or after the fact."

I sat frozen; my breath caught somewhere between my ribs and throat.

And then came the part I didn't expect.

"I used to blame you for the divorce," she said. "And I made you blame yourself, too. But it wasn't you, Daniel. Not really."

I looked at her. Her eyes were tired but clear.

"I was unhappy long before you knew. And I didn't let you in. I blamed you for being distant, but I was the one who shut the door first."

My chest tightened.

"You didn't fail me. We just couldn't fix what neither of us could name." She reached for my hand. "I wanted you to know that before I go. You deserved to be free of it."

We sat there for a long time in silence. There were no tears, not then. Just the weight of memory and unspoken things resting between us.

That night, I drove home in a fog. Izzy called just as I stepped through my front door.

"Hey, you," she said, her voice bright. "Missed hearing from you today."

I almost didn't answer.

Almost lied and said work had run late again. But I couldn't.

Instead, I said quietly, "Can we talk later? I had something come up."

She didn't push.

"Of course," she said softly. "Whenever you're ready."

I hung up and sank onto the couch.

My mind spun in a hundred directions.

Sandra was dying.

She had let go of blame and offered something like peace.

But rather than magically fixing everything, it left me spinning.

Because what if I had always been the one at fault and just didn't see it? What if I didn't deserve this second chance, this gentle, unfolding thing with Izzy?

Because what if happiness wasn't mine to claim anymore?

I closed my eyes and leaned back, hearing Sandra's voice echo in my memory: "You didn't fail me."

But I didn't know if I believed it yet.

Not fully.

All I knew was that for the first time in years, I was standing on the edge of something that felt like genuine happiness, and now, I wasn't sure if I was strong enough to hold on to it.

Should I pull back?

Should I just stop?

My mind was going to places I did not want it to go, but it did. I was pushing myself in many directions, thinking that all these years I had failed Sandra and didn't see her struggling; I had just thought of me. What a bastard I must have been in her eyes!

And yet, Sandra didn't see it that way.

"You didn't fail me."

Was it her last kindness to me to let me think that, or was it the truth?

Then my tears came out.

Slowly at first, then a bit more, for the woman I had spent 12 years of my life with. She was dying in a few days and had said to me: "You didn't fail me."

Maybe I didn't fail Sandra, but did I fail myself for not seeing her?

12

Pushing Away

Daniel

It took me three days to call Izzy.

Three days of rehearsing what to say. Of picking up my phone and putting it back down again. Of staring at her name in my contacts, my thumb hovering over "Call," like I was defusing a bomb.

I'd sent Izzy a text the night Sandra told me. "Something came up. I'll explain soon. I promise."

I should have called her, but I couldn't muster the energy.

She replied almost instantly: "I'm here when you're ready."

That hurt more than if she'd been angry.

Because I knew she meant it. And that's what made it harder.

I wasn't ready. Not really. But the longer I waited, the worse it felt.

On the third evening, after pacing my apartment like a caged animal, I finally called.

"Daniel," she said after the second ring, my name laced with both relief and concern.

"Hi," I managed, voice low.

"Are you okay?"

"No," I said, and then paused. "But I will be."

She said nothing right away, just gave me space.

"Can I come over?" I asked.

"Always."

Izzy's home smelled faintly of cinnamon and espresso beans, like the lingering ghost of a morning long gone. She opened the door barefoot, wearing jeans and an oversized sweater. No makeup. Hair tied in a messy knot.

God, she was beautiful.

She didn't ask questions as she let me in, just led me to the couch where we both sat, facing each other, legs folded beneath us like teenagers about to whisper secrets under blankets.

"It's Sandra," I said finally. "My ex-wife."

Izzy's face didn't shift.

No flicker of jealousy.

Just quiet listening.

"She called me out of the blue and asked me to come see her." I looked at my hands. They were trembling slightly. "She's dying."

Izzy reached for me, didn't say a word, just held my hand.

"She has this rare cancer: uterine sarcoma. No treatment left. A few weeks at most."

Izzy's thumb brushed gently over my knuckles. I hadn't realised I was squeezing her hand so tight.

"She told me the divorce wasn't my fault," I continued. "Said she had shut down long before I even realised there was something wrong."

I let out a hollow laugh.

"And for years, I blamed myself. I thought maybe I'd been emotionally absent, or too focused on work, or just not enough." I looked up at her, eyes stinging. "And now she's dying and giving me absolution I didn't even ask for. And I don't know what to do with it. I don't know what I'm supposed to feel."

Izzy didn't speak right away. She leaned in and rested her head against my shoulder.

"You feel what you feel," she murmured. "There's no right or wrong way to carry something like that."

We sat there for a while, not talking. Her warmth beside me was like a nice jumper, slowly quieting the panic that had taken up permanent residence in my chest.

Eventually, I said what I hadn't dared speak aloud yet. "After she told me, I started wondering if I even deserve this. You. This second chance."

Izzy lifted her head and looked at me, eyes fierce but kind.

"Daniel," she said softly, "we all carry our scars. Some we earned. Some were handed to us. But that you feel this deeply? That you're questioning it? That means you're already better than the man you think you were."

I swallowed hard. My throat burned.

"I don't want to hurt you," I said.

"Then don't," she said simply. "Just be here. Be you. Let me choose to stay, knowing all of it."

"You make it sound so simple."

"It's not," she said with a slight smile. "But it's worth it."

My chest tightened. Not with fear this time, but with hope.

We sat like that until the world outside went dark and the city quieted down. No promises were made. No declarations. Just an understanding: I wasn't alone in this.

Izzy stood and started toward the kitchen. "Let me make some tea."

"Izzy, please don't. I'll go now," was all I could say as I stood up and went to the door. I turn to look at her and, without saying a word, I closed the door behind me.

Izzy stood there and with a small tear running down her check she mumbled to herself, "He is pushing me away."

13

Don't Confuse the Past with the Future

Daniel

The days blurred.

I spent them between work and Sandra's apartment, which had taken on the quiet dread of a waiting room. The hospice nurse came and went with practiced calm. Miriam tried to keep the place feeling like a home; made soup, lit candles, opened the blinds, but the air was thick with the unspoken countdown.

Sandra was fading. Her body shrinking, her voice a whisper most days.

But her mind? Still sharp. Still capable of catching me off guard.

"You never look happier than when you talk about her," she said one morning, her voice raspy but steady.

"Who?"

She gave me that sideways smirk she used to wear when she beat me at cards. "Don't play dumb. Izzy."

I looked away. "That's over."

"No," she said. "It's paused. And maybe for a reason that feels noble to you, but don't confuse guilt with duty, Daniel. I've made my peace. You should too."

I didn't answer.

Just sat there holding her hand, the silence loud between us.

Later that night, I walked home instead of taking a cab. I needed the night air, the distance. My feet took me past The Velvet Note without my permission. Lights were on. People inside. I didn't stop.

Didn't even look through the window.

It had been nearly two weeks since I'd seen Izzy.

I'd called once. Left a message saying I was working things through.

She didn't call back, and I didn't blame her.

I had pulled away so fast, it probably looked like I'd never really wanted her in the first place.

But I did.

God help me, I did.

And every day I didn't go to her felt like a betrayal.

But every day I didn't go to Sandra felt like abandonment.

So, I chose the one who was leaving. The one who wouldn't be here much longer. The one I could bury, along with my guilt.

Until Ryan showed up.

He let himself into my apartment like he always had, arms full of takeaway and attitude.

"Jesus, Daniel," he said, tossing me a container of fried rice. "You look like a rejected Dickens character."

I ignored him and went and sat at the kitchen table. He sat across from me and dug into his noodles like it was a normal day.

"Izzy called me," he said after a while.

I looked up, startled. "She did?"

"She was worried. Said you disappeared. Thought maybe something had happened."

"She's not wrong."

"You should call her."

"I have, but I can't talk to her right now."

Ryan dropped his chopsticks with a snap. "Bullshit."

"I'm dealing with something."

"And what exactly are you not dealing with by avoiding her?"

I stood up and walked to the sink. My stomach churned. "It's complicated."

"No, it's not." His voice rose. "You love someone who loves your stupid arse back. And yeah, your ex-wife is dying. That's horrible. But you don't fix it by punishing yourself and pushing away the one person who makes you feel alive again."

I turned, anger bubbling. "You don't understand."

"No, I do. More than you think. You're afraid. Do you think if you let yourself be happy, it means you didn't care enough about Sandra? But that's not grief, man. That's guilt. And it's going to eat you alive if you let it."

I stared at him, breathing hard. "She's dying, Ryan."

"And she wants you to live."

I sat back down. The weight of it all crashed into me.

"I'm afraid I'll ruin it again."

"Then don't. Learn from it. Talk. Be honest. Show up." He softened. "You deserve a shot at joy, Daniel. Even now. Especially now."

The silence stretched between us. Then Ryan stood and slapped a hand on my shoulder.

"You're not the man you were with, Sandra. And Izzy's not her either. Don't confuse the past with the present."

I looked at him, something breaking open inside me. And for the first time in many days, I let myself cry.

14

Her Side of the Story

Daniel

Of course, it had to be a grey afternoon for the funeral.

The sky hung heavy above the cemetery, all muted clouds and wind that couldn't decide if it wanted to rain or not. I stood near the back, away from the closer circle of mourners. Miriam, a few of Sandra's cousins, two colleagues from her workdays. They huddled together like the grief itself had a centre, and I was just orbiting it now.

I couldn't remember what the priest said. Something about peace. Something about release.

I kept my eyes on the casket.

Sandra looked small in that box.

It made little sense.

She had always been larger than life. Sharp-witted, unafraid of her opinions, the type of woman who wore dark lipstick to brunch and read poetry aloud when no one asked her to.

And now she was just gone.

When the funeral was over, people drifted off slowly, murmuring condolences, laying a hand on my arm, offering tight smiles that said everything and nothing.

I lingered, staring at the stone they hadn't carved yet, when a woman in a navy-blue coat approached me. I knew the face, but not the name. One of Izzy's friends, I was sure of it. She'd been at the Velvet Note once, laughing with her, leaning over the bar.

She smiled softly, but there was something knowing in her eyes.

"I'm sorry about your loss," she said gently.

"Thank you."

She paused, glancing toward the flowers laid out on the grave. "Izzy wanted to be here. But she thought maybe you needed space."

I swallowed hard.

Her name felt like a stone skipping across a frozen lake inside my chest.

"Tell her I understand," I said.

The woman tilted her head, looking at me a little too carefully. "I will. But I hope you know she's been here before."

That caught me.

"What do you mean?"

"She loved someone once," she said, quiet now. "Really loved him. He left before she ever got the chance to say it. Just disappeared. Said he couldn't handle it, or he wasn't ready, or whatever excuse people use when they're scared."

I said nothing. I didn't have to.

"She won't chase you, Daniel," she added. "She's not that girl anymore. And I don't think she should have to be."

That stayed with me. Hit me in the gut harder than I was ready for.

She gave me a small, almost wistful smile. "I hope you figure out what you want before it's too late."

And just like that, she was gone, blending into the retreating mourners like she'd never said a word.

I didn't even know her name, so I just stood there a while longer. Long enough for the wind to finally push out a few drops of rain. Long enough to feel them soak into my jacket. Long enough to realise the ache in my chest had less to do with Sandra and more to do with the space Izzy had left behind.

Because she had left.

She'd stopped texting.

Stopped calling.

She hadn't come to the funeral, and even if I understood it, even if I respected it, it still cut deep.

I had disappeared from her life when things got heavy. Just like the man before me.

That was Izzy's side of her story.

And now if I wanted her.

If I wanted us, I'd have to do something terrifying.

I'd have to show up.

15

The Velvet Note

Daniel

I had never walked faster to the Velvet Note.

No hesitation this time, no circling the block, no manufactured errands or phone calls that could distract me. Just me, coat collar up against the wind, heart hammering, gut twisted in that familiar way that said I might be too late.

But it didn't matter anymore. I had to try.

The moment I stepped inside, I knew Izzy wasn't there.

The place was quieter than usual; midweek, post rush, and behind the bar, with his sleeves rolled and polishing a glass like some kind of sitcom bartender cliché, stood Freddy.

He spotted me immediately and gave a slow, neutral smile. I walked up, trying to act casual, but everything about me screamed with urgency.

"Hey," I said.

"Hey yourself," Freddy replied, leaning on the bar. "You look like you've been through the wringer."

I huffed. "Something like that."

Freddy studied me for a moment. He had Izzy's eyes, but where hers held warmth like a candle flickering in jazz blue shadows, his were sharper, cautious. Protective.

"You're looking for her," he said. Not a question.

"Yeah."

"She's not here."

I nodded, not sure what to say next, so I asked, "Do you know where she is?"

"No, I don't, but she's okay," Freddy added, almost like he could see the panic that flared in my chest. "Just needed a break."

"From the café?"

"From all of it, I think."

There was a long silence between us, filled with the low hum of jazz and the clinking of cutlery in the back. Then Freddy stepped out from behind the bar and reached under it.

"I figured you might show up eventually," he said, pulling out a sealed envelope and placing it gently on the bar. "She asked me to give you this."

I stared at it. "Do I read it here?"

Freddy shook his head. "She said to read it away from the café. Alone."

My hand hovered over the envelope, but I didn't pick it up just yet.

"What's in it?" I asked.

He shrugged. "Not my story to tell, nor my business."

"You know," I said, trying for a smile, "you're kind of intimidating for a jazz bartender."

"Good," he said, grin sharp. "Means I'm doing my job."

I finally took the envelope.

It was heavy, like it held more than just paper, like it carried the weight of weeks, of hesitation, of a lot of almosts.

"Thanks," I said.

Freddy gave me a nod. "Don't wait too long."

I didn't open it right away.

I took the long way home.

Sat with the envelope on the passenger seat like it might bite me. Even after I got inside and tossed my keys in the bowl, I still didn't read it. I poured myself a glass of scotch, turned off the lights, and settled into the darkness, lit by only a single lamp. Went to my desk with the drink and I stared at the note like it was going to detonate.

It was fear.

I knew that.

Not of rejection. Not exactly.

It was fear that she'd moved on.

That she'd seen through me, through my cowardice, and written me off.

That I had waited too long.

Hours passed.

Midnight came and went.

The street outside went still. I couldn't avoid it anymore.

I opened the envelope.

Her handwriting was the first thing I saw: elegant, confident, slanted slightly to the right. Just like her.

Daniel,

I've rewritten this a dozen times. Maybe more. I'm not great at letting people see me, not when it counts. You're not the only one who knows how to run. I've done my fair share of vanishing acts too. But I've spent too many years waiting for love to stay. Waiting for someone to stop leaving before I could say, "Don't."

I won't wait for you, Daniel. I can't. But I'll be here if you decide to stop running.

Izzy

That was it.

No anger.

No plea.

Just an invitation.

And the thing that gutted me, the thing that filled my lungs like air after a deep, hard dive, was that she still believed in something worth staying for.

She just would not beg for it.

I folded the letter carefully and pressed it to my chest, as if by some quiet magic that could bring her closer.

"I'm done running," I said to the empty apartment.

And I meant it.

16

Realisation

Daniel

I couldn't sleep.

Izzy's letter sat on the nightstand like it had a heartbeat.

Every time I closed my eyes, her words echoed in my head:

'I won't wait for you, Daniel. I can't. But I'll be here if you decide to stop running.'

I had stopped running.

But now she was gone.

I sat up, grabbed my phone, and stared at my contacts.

How many of her friends did I actually know?

Zero. That's how many.

I considered calling Freddy, but something told me that wouldn't go well. He'd already done me one favour by giving me the letter; I wasn't sure I could expect more.

Ryan, though?

Ryan was my chaos specialist.

And if there was ever a time, I needed chaos to bend in my favour, it was now.

I called him at 2:14 a.m.

"Daniel?" His voice was groggy. "You better be in jail or on fire."

"Izzy's gone."

Pause. "Like gone? Gone?"

"She left. Freddy gave me a note. She's not at the café, and I don't know where she is."

"Well, damn." He yawned. "You finally admitted to yourself that you're in love with her, didn't you?"

"I think so."

"You think so?"

"I read her letter four times, cried during one of them, and now I'm calling you in the middle of the night because I need to find her."

"Yeah, that's love." He exhaled. "All right, Watson. Let's find your jazz girl." There was a pause as he thought. "Which of her friends did you call first? Women often go to other women to share things."

I kept silent.

"Hello, Daniel? You there? Did we disconnect?"

"Ryan, I have no contacts for her."

"None?"

"None."

"Well, you are worthless. Am I on your contact list?"

"Yes, of course."

"Just checking. OK, what time does the Velvet Note open?"

"You don't know?"

"No, Daniel, that is why I am asking you. You should know. You been dating the owner now for six months."

I had no freaking idea.

I never been there in the morning. If I stayed late with Izzy, she locked up and went home. Someone else had to open the café.

"Let me look it up. Hang on."

I open a new tab and find the website.

In bright white letters at the bottom of the home page were the operating hours: 6:00 a.m.

"Ryan, it opens early at 6:00 a.m."

"Too early for me. Let's meet there at 10:30 a.m. That way we miss the early birds that go in for coffee, the breakfast crowd, and the mid-morning java enthusiasts. We can ask more civilised questions then."

"No, Ryan. I want to be there early. To get started in searching for Izzy."

Silence on the other side of the line.

"Daniel. Do you have any idea on what questions to ask? Where to start? Who to ask?"

Silence on my side of the line.

"No, I do not."

"Then let me handle the questions. You buy the coffee when we get there. See you at 10:30 a.m. at The Velvet Note."

I showed up at 10:30 a.m. at the café wearing clothes and a determination that probably made me look as if I had a hangover.

Freddy was behind the counter working the barista station. A few other young servers were working the counter/bar or serving tables. He saw me and sighed like he knew this was coming.

"I need to find her," I said.

"I figured," he replied, calmly making an expresso.

Just then, Ryan walked in.

"Good morning, everyone. Lovely morning. Top of the morning to you, Freddy."

"Good morning, Ryan. Your usual?"

"Yes, please, and a few minutes of your time when you bring it to my table. Make it two. Daniel will have the same."

"What the hell, Ryan? I was asking Freddy questions…"

But Ryan grabbed my arms and pulled me over to a corner table.

"Sit. Shut up. Drink your coffee when it arrives. I'll handle it. No, what did you ask Freddy?"

"I told him I needed to find her."

"And?"

"I was about to ask him for her surname when you walked in."

"YOU DON'T KNOW HER SURNAME?"

"Well, I don't think so. No, I don't know her last name."

"She gave it to you," he said. "You just weren't listening."

"Laurant. Right." I blinked.

Just then Freddy walked up with two concoctions that looked like coffee.

I looked at my cup and asked, "What's this?"

Freddy smiled and explained. "This is Ryan's favourite morning brew. We call it the Velvet Bom Ryan in his honour. A dark roasted double espresso with condensed milk at the bottom."

No way I was having that.

"Freddy," Ryan interjected. "Got a moment for a question or two?"

"Of course I do for you, Ryan. What's up?"

"My dear friend seems to have misplaced Izzy and needs to find her. Do you happen to know where she is?"

He paused. "She didn't want anyone chasing her."

"Freddy, please."

Freddy looked at Ryan, then studied me for a moment. Then he sighed and reached into his apron. "She left this here a few days ago."

It was a postcard. Blank on the back, but the image was of a rocky shoreline. No text. No address.

"Any idea where this is?"

He shook his head. "But you're resourceful, right, Ryan?"

"I once got locked out of my apartment and used a pool noodle and a spatula to break in."

"You're halfway there."

"Thanks, Freddy. You are a gentleman and a genius with coffee."

As Freddy went back behind the counter, I asked Ryan why he came. I could have asked the same question and gotten the same answer.

"No, my boy, you would not have. You see, Freddy told me he liked you, but once you broke his sister's heart, you are in the dump with him. So, you are welcome."

"So now what?"

"Just follow me."

Finishing that monstrosity named the Velvet Bom Ryan, both Ryan and I grabbed a taxi, and we headed into the central business district, before we stopped in front of a travel agency.

We walked in and Ryan approached a young female travel agent behind the desk, laid the postcard on it and asked, "Young lady, do you know where this is?"

The employee blinked at Ryan. "Is this… homework?"

"No. It's personal."

She studied the photo. "Looks like… I don't know, maybe Kiama? Could be Bombo Beach?"

"Are you sure?"

"Nope."

Ryan grabbed the postcard and looked at me. "Follow me." We walked out the door and headed into a coffee shop next door.

"Now what?"

"Time for a coffee."

"We just had a coffee."

"No, I had a Velvet Bom Ryan now it is time for a latte."

So, we ordered one latte and waited for it to come to our table.

"Give me your phone," Ryan commanded.

I obeyed as a peasant and handed him my phone.

Five minutes later, he handed it back to me, stating he had added me to a Facebook group for coastal photography and uploaded the image, pretending I was a travel blogger.

Ten minutes later, someone commented, Pretty sure that's Long Gully Point. Near Gerroa.

Jackpot!

"Great. Let's go back to my place." I stood. "I'll pack a quick bag and then drive you to your place so you can also pack, and then we are off to Long Gully Point."

"Whoa, Sherlock. You are packing and going. I have nothing else to do here."

I took a moment to think about how to say what was next. "Ryan, everything you have done and asked what I could have done? What makes it so special that you did it?"

"My boy, it's simple. It is how I do it and say it. I am marvellous."

Back at home, I packed nothing more than the postcard, my toothbrush, and three days of clean clothes.

I stopped at every café in every coastal town along the way that vaguely resembled the photo, just in case the Facebook post might have been mistaken.

One café owner in Berry told me I looked "romantically dishevelled."

Another in Gerringong asked if I was "searching for a spiritual connection."

"No," I replied. "Just a jazz singer with a fondness for metaphors and caffeine."

The guy nodded solemnly. "Aren't we all?"

The breakthrough came from the most unlikely source: a fisherman named Kevin.

I was walking along a path near the beach at Gerroa, holding the postcard like a dowsing rod, when I saw a man cleaning his nets.

"You lost?" he asked, not unkindly.

"Sort of. I'm looking for someone."

"Aren't we all?"

I showed him the only selfie of Izzy and me and asked if he has seen her.

"Ah, yes. She's staying up the road."

My heart nearly leapt out of my throat. "What?"

"Yeah. Surname Laurant, I think. She came in for coffee two days ago at our local coffee shop. Said she used to sing. Pretty eyes. Nice figure. Likes her solitude."

I was stunned. "Where is she staying?"

"A cabin overlooking the water, I believe. Go up the track, past the surf shed. Third one with the green roof."

I thanked him profusely. I almost hugged him. I think I might've cried a little.

Then I ran.

The cabin was quiet.

I stood outside for a good ten minutes before I had the nerve to knock. I practiced what I'd say at least four times.

But when the door opened, all that vanished.

Izzy was there, wearing a loose sweater and no makeup. Her hair was tied back in a messy bun, and she looked like the most beautiful thing I'd ever seen.

She froze when she saw me. "Daniel?"

"Hi," I said, breathless.

She said nothing.

"I got your note," I continued. "I didn't read it right away. I was scared. But I read it. And I, I'm here. I came."

"Why?"

"Because I've been an idiot."

She waited for more.

"I didn't know how to hold on to something good. Not after Sandra. And then Sandra, she came back into my life just to say goodbye. And it reminded me of everything I thought I had failed at. And you, you were starting to feel like everything I didn't deserve."

Izzy's eyes softened, but she still didn't speak.

"I wanted to be brave," I said. "But I didn't know how. Until now. Until you."

A long silence.

Then, softly: "How did you find me?"

"Internet stalking. Some possible harassment of a young travel agent, a lot of coffee, and a fisherman named Kevin."

Her mouth twitched. "Kevin has a pleasant smile and knows how to recommend an excellent coffee."

"Better than Velvet Bon Ryan?" I asked.

"Goodness, yes," she replied. "But his conversation is five-star."

I smiled, and she laughed. A small, reluctant, beautiful laugh.

"I'm sorry I left like that," she said.

"I understand. I pushed you away. I let my fear decide for me."

"Are you still afraid?"

I stepped closer. "Yes. But I'm here, anyway."

She looked at me for a long time. Then she turned slightly, opened the door wider.

"You want some coffee?"

"I'd prefer a beer."

She raised an eyebrow. "Since when do you drink beer?"

"Since Ryan shoved a Velvet Bon Ryan down my throat," I said solemnly.

She smiled then. "Come in."

The cabin smelled like sea salt and pine. She had books everywhere, a guitar by the window, and a half-filled sketchbook on the table.

We sat across from each other on the couch. She holds a warm mug of coffee and me a Great Northern Super Crisp she had in the fridge.

For a while, neither of us spoke.

The silence wasn't uncomfortable. It was…tentative.

Like a first note before the song begins.

"I meant what I said in the letter," Izzy finally said. "I won't chase anyone again. I've done it too many times."

"You shouldn't have to."

"I want to be with someone who shows up. Not just in grand gestures, but in the ordinary ways."

I nodded. "I want to be that someone. For you."

"And what about everything else? Your guilt? Your grief?"

"They're still there. But they don't get to steer anymore."

Izzy watched me carefully, her eyes studying every word like it was a lyric she hadn't heard before. Then she reached across the space between us and took my hand.

"Okay," she said softly.

"Okay?"

"We'll start here. With coffee, beer, and honesty."

"That sounds like a jazz album."

She smiled. "Maybe it will be."

Later, we walked along the beach as the sun dipped low, casting gold across the waves.

Izzy slipped her arm through mine.

No fireworks.

No sweeping declarations.

Just a shared silence that meant everything.

As we watched the tide roll in, I realised something.

Sometimes love didn't arrive with thunder.

Sometimes it just… stayed.

And now, so was I.

17

A Night of Love

Izzy

The sound of the ocean slipped into the cabin like a lullaby as I opened the door. It felt like a soft, rhythmic, rocking mood. I lit a small candle on the window ledge, more out of habit than for light. The moon was already doing its share of the work, spilling silver across the room and turning the cabin into something otherworldly, something sacred.

Daniel had gone quiet again.

Not the uncomfortable kind. It was something else. That pause he had, when he was deep in thought, trying to work through something he couldn't quite put words to yet.

He stood near the little bookshelf, fingertips brushing over the spines, looking at all the titles. His shoulders were softer now than they were that afternoon when he first appeared at my door. Even so, there was a weight on him. It clung to him like shadows he'd learned to live with.

I let the silence stretch between us a bit longer. I'd spent too many years filling spaces that weren't mine to fill. If he needed time to breathe, I'd give him all the air in the world. I knew what I wanted tonight, but did he?

When he finally turned to face me, I saw it in his eyes; that flicker of something raw, something deep. Love. Longing, maybe even fear. All tangled together like vines climbing up the side of a house.

"Izzy," he said quietly, "I need you to know I don't want to rush this."

"I know."

He hesitated. "It's not because I don't want you. God knows I do; that's not it at all. It's just that I want to get it right. I want to build something."

The vulnerability in his voice struck a chord deep in me. So many men had chased me, wanted me, praised my beauty, my voice, my fire. They'd bedded me, but they had all run when things got still. When the music stopped, they didn't know how to stay.

But Daniel was trying to stay.

I took off my shoes and crossed the room slowly, barefoot on the wooden floor, until I stopped in front of him. "Then let's go slow," I said. "Let's take our time."

He exhaled like that was the only permission he needed.

I reached up, gently touching the collar of his shirt, smoothing it down. Then I let my fingers trace the line of his jaw, where the stubble had started to grow. He leaned into the touch, almost imperceptibly.

"Come with me," I whispered, taking his hand.

And he did.

The bedroom was lit with the light from the moon; soft shadows moved across the walls from the moonbeams shining through the light curtains. They seemed to dance too. I continue to lead him in by the hand. Nothing urgent, nothing showy. Just two people stepping into something honest.

He stopped at the doorway.

"Izzy, are you sure?"

I nodded. "I want to be seen, Daniel. Not just touched."

"I see you," he said, voice thick.

I reached for him again, this time with both hands, pulling him gently into the room. The weight he carried all this time didn't need to vanish, it just needed somewhere to rest.

We stood at the edge of the bed, and for a moment, all we did was look at each other. I let myself memorise his face. The softness in his eyes. The small furrow between his brows that told me he was holding more than he spoke. The way he watched me like he was afraid I might disappear.

I moved first, fingers brushing the buttons of his shirt. He caught my hand for a second, still unsure.

"I've been through a lot," he whispered.

"I know," I replied. "We both have."

His hands came up then, not rushed, but with reverence. He touched my cheek like he was making sure I was real, and then his palm cradled the back of my neck as he kissed me.

Slow. Gentle. Not a storm, but a soft tide caressing me.

It deepened gradually, with breaths exchanged and hearts learning each other's rhythm. He touched me like he was listening, like my skin spoke to him, reacting to his touch, letting him know I understand.

We moved to the bed like it wasn't about sex.

It was about arriving.

About being seen without shame.

About healing through closeness, not escaping with it.

He undressed me the way one would open a gift they'd been waiting for all their life. I undressed him with quiet wonder, seeing a man, not just a body, one who had scars not just on his heart, but etched in the way he held himself.

There was tenderness in every movement, like we both knew how fragile this was.

When he finally entered me, it wasn't lust that drove us; it was a longing.

A longing to be known.

A longing to be safe.

A longing to matter to someone who wouldn't walk away when the song ended.

He moved gently, eyes never leaving mine, and I let myself open in a way I hadn't in years. I let myself feel not just pleasure, but love.

Safety.

Intimacy.

And he felt it too.

I could see it in the way his hands trembled as he held my face. On the way, his breath hitched when I whispered his name like a secret.

"Daniel."

In the way we moved together, no rush, no choreography, just a raw and real connection.

It was a kind of love and passion I hadn't known before. A kind that didn't burn too fast or consume everything in its path. It glowed. It lingered.

And afterward, when we lay tangled in the sheets, hearts still beating out of our chests like long distant drums, Daniel turned to me, his voice barely audible.

"I didn't know it could feel like this."

"Like what?" I asked.

"Like you."

A lump rose in my throat. I brushed his hair back from his forehead, kissed the crease between his brows, and smiled.

"That's because we're not just loving," I whispered. "We're trusting again."

We drifted into sleep sometime after that, his arms around me, my back against his chest. The night was quiet except for the waves outside and the occasional creak of the cabin settling.

But something inside me had settled too.

Daniel hadn't just returned to me.

He had chosen to.

And for the first time in a very long time, I wasn't waiting for love to stay.

It was already here.

And damn it, I knew that this time it wasn't going anywhere.

18

Back to Reality

Izzy

The morning light poured in through the bedroom window, all soft and golden, casting little shadows as the light rays filtered through the slim window curtains across the wooden floor. I could see from the bed that the sea was quieter today. I turned over in the bed; the sheets were cool on my skin and found Daniel lying there with one arm slung across his chest, eyes open, staring at the ceiling.

He looked peaceful. And yet, there was a flicker in his gaze, like thoughts were bouncing around his mind.

I reached out and let my fingers skim his forearm. He turned to look at me and smiled, slow and sleepy, the kind of look that made me feel yummy.

"Morning," I said softly.

"Morning," he echoed.

We lay there for a while, not speaking, letting the weight of the night settle in our bones. It was lovely. It was real. And it was just the beginning of something neither of us had planned for.

Eventually, I shifted, pulling the blanket up and resting my head against his shoulder.

"You're thinking too loud," I teased gently.

He chuckled, but it wasn't the carefree kind. "Just reality knocking on the door."

"Yeah," I murmured. "I figure."

Silence again.

But this one wasn't awkward. It was pregnant with questions.

I lifted myself up slightly, resting on one elbow to face him. "We should talk, shouldn't we?"

Daniel nodded. "Yes, we should."

I sat up and pulled on the oversized shirt I'd worn last night and strolled into the kitchen barefoot to make some coffee. Daniel followed, grabbing one of the flannel throws from the armchair and wrapping it around his waist like a makeshift kilt.

We were ridiculous. But in the best possible way.

The kettle boiled, the smell of fresh grounds filled the air, and I asked what he might want for breakfast.

"Oh, sweetie. Anything you make will be good."

My goodness, he called me sweetie. This must be getting serious indeed, I thought.

I quickly made a couple of over easy eggs; some toast and poured the coffee as we sat at the little round table. It was by the open window, and we listened to the hum of the ocean as we enjoyed our food.

We finished and Daniel cleaned up before he brought back two more steaming mugs of coffee. We both took a sip before either of us said a word.

Then he exhaled and began. "Izzy, I've never had a morning like this before."

I smiled. "Neither have I."

"But I also know love doesn't exist in a vacuum. Not for people like us. We come with history."

"Baggage, you mean?" I offered with a raised brow.

He grinned. "Yes. Overhead luggage, checked bags, emotional carry-ons."

We both laughed softly.

Then the moment shifted again.

"I have to go back home to Sydney tomorrow," he said. "Work is already waiting, and I can't avoid it forever."

"I know," I replied. "And the café won't run itself."

We sipped again. Then Daniel set his cup down carefully and leaned forward.

"Izzy, I don't want to mess this up. I've messed things up before, especially with Sandra, and I know I've still got things to work through. But I'm not walking away from this. Not unless you tell me to."

My heart squeezed at that. "I don't want you to walk away, Daniel. I want to see where this goes. But you're right. We need to talk about what comes next."

He nodded. "So, how do you want to do this? Weekly train rides and awkward calendars?"

I laughed, but I knew he wasn't entirely joking.

"We figure it out," I said. "Step by step."

"Okay," he said. "Then let's really talk."

I appreciated that about Daniel. He wasn't afraid to go deep. He just needed the right space. The right time.

I reached across the table and laced my fingers through his.

"Let's start with the hard stuff," I offered. "Finances. What does life look like for you right now?"

Daniel rubbed the back of his neck. "Honestly? Pretty stable. Unit is paid for and worth probably $1.3 to $1.5

million. I've got a good—actually a great job with a fantastic company running several projects. The occasional outside seminars present me with an opportunity for extra cash for speaking engagements, both internal for the company and externally for clients. Remember, I just did one in Melbourne. The company has an international seminar once a year overseas that brings me extra exposure as well. Personally, I hope to get started in writing again. I am feeling, well, more complete now. To be honest, I am not rolling in it. My super is strong; if the market doesn't have a big hiccup, I should retire at a reasonably young age."

"Really? How young would that be?"

"Oh, say 60 to 62."

"I'm okay too," I said. "The Velvet Note is paid in full. No mortgage on the building. All bills current. I own my home and this cabin. As you can see, it's a palace, right?"

Daniel smiled.

"It is to me," he said.

"If I were to sell the jazz café, it could fetch over $3 million simply for the land and location. The house is worth easily $2 million to $2.4 million. The cabin I wouldn't sell. It is a palace."

Daniel chuckled at that and nodded.

I continued, "The Velvet Note pays for itself and then some. I've got a small inheritance from my aunt which is tied up in a term deposit ladder, and my super should allow me to retire OK. But running a café isn't exactly a goldmine."

We exchanged knowing smiles. Neither of us were chasing wealth. But we were also both aware love didn't pay for leaky roofs or groceries.

"I don't need anyone to rescue me," I added. "And I'm not here to fix anyone, either."

"I wouldn't ask you to," he said quietly. "I just want to build something equally."

There it was again.

That thread between us.

Stronger than yesterday. Woven even tighter now.

"What about previous commitments?" I asked. "Other than Ryan barging into every moment of your life."

He laughed. "That's an occupational hazard, yes. But no, nothing serious. I don't have kids. No aging parents to look after. What about you?"

"My mother is in Queensland," I said. "I visit her once a year. Still has all her marbles and always asking me question about my paramours. Hope you're ready for that."

This time Daneil let out a loud crackle.

"To finish up, I don't have kids either. Just the café, and course, my younger brother Freddy."

"I like him," Daniel said with a grin.

I smirked. "You were ready to fight him, admit it, and he is pissed at you for what happened."

He held up his hands. "Okay, okay. I panicked. But he earned my respect, and I will make it up to him. Promise."

"Good. You'll need it," I said. "Freddy can smell bad intentions a mile away."

Daniel leaned back in his chair. "That's fair."

I finished my coffee and let the warm ceramic rest between my palms. "What about your dreams, Daniel? What do you want now?"

He looked down at his mug, thinking.

"I want peace," he said finally. "Not the absence of chaos, but the kind of peace that feels like home. I want to start writing and keep writing. Maybe retire early. Travel a bit more and write. Have someone to share it with."

Then his eyes met mine. "And you?"

I bit my bottom lip. "I want to be seen. Really seen. I've lived a loud life, Daniel. Music. Performance. But I want quiet now. Honest connections. A life where I can wake up next to someone and not wonder if they're going to leave."

His gaze softened.

"I'm not going to leave," he said.

"I believe you," I whispered.

We stood, cups empty and hearts full. I reached up and touched his face again, letting my thumb trail along the crease near his eye.

"We'll go slow," I said. "But we'll go."

He kissed my forehead. "I'm all in."

"OK, we know all the necessary background on each of us, so let's go and pack and head back to reality."

19

Sydney Skyline

Izzy

The cabin behind us felt like a tucked-away chapter in a book neither of us wanted to close, but we knew the pages had to keep turning. The car was packed; the windows rolled down to let in the salt air, and the early sun glinted off the winding coastal road ahead.

"Izzy," Daniel asked as we drove off, "how did you get here, anyway? I never saw a vehicle."

"I took the train."

"Really? I didn't know the line would come down this far."

"It does, and it goes further. You should try it one time."

"I will," he said.

We said little after that, and the silence that followed was exactly right. The good kind.

Daniel drove, one hand on the wheel, the other resting gently on my thigh, like a tether. We played jazz. Some old Miles Davis, some Chet Baker, and let the music speak for a while.

About an hour down the road, my stomach betrayed me with a very audible growl.

Daniel glanced over, grinning. "Did you just roar at me?"

"I did not roar. That was a sophisticated lady rumble."

"Well, your sophisticated lady rumble is telling me we need to eat."

We pulled into a sleepy little coastal town that looked like it had more seagulls than people and spotted a crooked sign that read "The Cranky Pelican — Est. 1974." We exchanged glances.

"I'm sold," I said.

Inside, it was all nautical kitsch.

Nets on the ceiling, faded photographs of long-gone fishing boats, and the faint scent of yesterday's chowder still lingering in the air. A stout, red-faced man behind the bar looked up from a crossword puzzle and greeted us with a booming, "Well, look at you two lovebirds!"

I nearly tripped over a stool. Daniel chuckled and nodded politely. "Just looking for some lunch."

"Newlyweds, eh?" the man said with a wink. "You've got that just married glow. We see it all the time around here. Something in the sea air, I suppose."

I opened my mouth to correct him, but Daniel beat me to it.

"Oh yeah," he said, slapping a hand over his heart dramatically, "we're still in the honeymoon phase. She even lets me drive sometimes."

The man roared with laughter and waved us toward a table by the window. "First drink is on the house for the happy couple!"

As we sat down, I leaned over and whispered, "You are insufferable."

"Please, Mrs Carter," he said in a prim tone, "not in public."

I slapped his arm, trying not to laugh. "I will pour soup on you."

We shared a basket of fish and chips and a couple of ginger beers.

Between bites and giggles, I watched Daniel in the sunlight, the soft crinkles at the corners of his eyes, the way he asked the server for extra napkins for me without being asked. It was ridiculous, perfect, and awkward and everything I never knew I needed.

Back on the road, the lightness lingered, but the tone slowly turned more serious. Sydney loomed ahead like a bookmark in a story we had to return to. Daniel cleared his throat.

"So," he began, "what does this look like realistically?"

I took a breath. "We're both tied to our work. The café's my life. And I know you love your job."

"I do," he said. "But I could ask to shift to more consulting work, which will reduce my workload. On a demand sort of specialty. Come and go when I please. Take the seminars that are better for me, for us."

He continued after a moment to think.

"It's not ideal, but it gives me some flexibility. Maybe a few days a week at home with you. A few in the office or with the client. Or… even at Long Gully Point, if you wish?"

I looked at him. "You'd do that?"

"I'd try," he said. "Because this… you… matter."

I felt a tug in my chest. "Maybe I bring in another manager to the café. Take a couple of days off each week. It's not impossible. It'll be a juggle, but we've both danced on tighter wires before."

"Have you thought of selling the place to Freddy?"

Izzy thought about that for a moment. "No, I have not. Let me think more about that."

We drove on, talking about trivial things: shared calendars, who was the better cook (him, annoyingly), and how neither of us were morning people but somehow managed to fake it when needed. We talked about how to tell the people in our lives.

"Freddy's going to pretend to be cool about it but then absolutely grill you behind the espresso machine."

Daniel smirked. "I'm counting on it. I owe him that much."

"And Ryan?" I asked.

"He's going to be unbearable."

"Wasn't he already?"

Daniel laughed. "Fair point."

Then I hesitated. "My mother…"

Daniel grew quiet.

"She's not unkind," I intoned. "But she's blunt. She once told Freddy his hair made him look like a sad llama. She'll say things."

He smiled. "I've handled CEOs and their committees. I can handle an opinionated woman."

"She's French-Australian," I warned.

Daniel's eyebrows rose. "So, I should bring wine."

"Superb wine," I said. "And maybe a cheese plate."

We both laughed, but underneath the humour was a shared understanding this was getting really real. We were weaving our lives into something new. Thread by thread.

As Sydney's skyline came into view, I reached across and laced my fingers through his again.

"You're not running anymore," I said.

He looked at me, eyes gentle. "No. I'm walking forward with you."

20

The Dance We Never Had

Izzy

I had been staring at my phone for five minutes.

It wasn't that I didn't want to call Freddy. It was that, for once, I didn't know exactly how he'd react.

He had been protective ever since we were kids.

When Dad left, Freddy stepped in at fourteen years old and was suddenly the man of the house. He never stopped being that. Even now, slinging lattes and organising jazz nights at the Velvet Note, he watched over me like a hawk in a well-fitted apron.

And I was the older sibling. Go figure.

And Daniel, well, Daniel was a shift in my universe.

I tapped the contact and hit the call button.

"Evening, sis," Freddy answered, already chewing on something. "How are things where you are?"

"You're eating again?" I teased.

"Always. Vegemite toast. Classic. Getting ready for tonight's gig. What's going on?"

I took a breath. "Can you come to my place tomorrow? Around 11? Daniel and I want to talk to you."

There was a pause.

"Daniel? Did he find you? Did he upset you?"

"No. Everything's OK. Can you make it?"

"For a talk? Like…a talk?"

"Not that kind of talk," I blurted. "No babies, no weddings, no emergencies. Just a conversation."

Freddy exhaled a long, performative sigh. "Fine. I'll cancel my juggling class."

"You do not juggle."

"You don't know my life, Isabelle."

"Eleven."

He softened. "Of course. I'll call Beatrix right now and ask her to come in and sub." There was a pause, then – "Are you okay, Izzy?"

"I am," I said, surprised at how true that felt. "I truly, really am."

Daniel

Meanwhile, in my apartment, I sat with my thumb hovering over Ryan's contact like it was a nuclear launch button.

Ryan was my best mate, but he was also the nosiest person on Earth, and I knew he was going to milk this moment for all it was worth.

I tapped the call button.

"Ah! The prodigal consultant returns!" Ryan answered with no hello, just drama. "What's it been, two weeks? Did you move to Spain? Join a cult? Get abducted by aliens who serve coffee with notes attached?"

"I was gone three days, Ryan. And I'm seeing Izzy again."

There was a pause.

"No shit? She took you back?"

"No shit, and she did take me back. We are in a better place, let's say."

"Well, thank God. I was about to file a missing person's report under 'emotional cowardice.'"

"Feel better now?"

"Much. What's up?"

"I'd like you to come over to Izzy's place tomorrow. 11. Just you, me, Izzy and her brother Freddy."

"Ooh, a summit," Ryan said. "Should I bring a tie and a PowerPoint?"

I laughed. "Just yourself."

He paused again, then added with rare sincerity, "Glad you're back, mate. She's good for you."

"Yeah," I said. "I think I'm finally good for me too."

21

Friendship Cyclone

"Did someone say there'd be carbs and unresolved tension?" Ryan's voice announced even before the door opened all the way.

He barrelled in like a sitcom character arriving mid scene, arms wide, sunglasses on indoors for reasons known only to him. He caught sight of Freddy holding the bakery bag and pointed dramatically.

"Aha! Croissants! I knew I smelled baked peace offerings. That's how you know something big about to go down. Where's my seat? I call the ottoman! It gives me the emotional height advantage."

He plopped down with a flourish, only to immediately sink too low into the cushion. "This ottoman just rejected me. Rude."

Izzy barely stifled a grin.

Freddy sighed.

Daniel rubbed his temples like he regretted every decision that led to this moment.

Ryan reached for a croissant. "No butter? What is this, the post-apocalypse?"

"Ryan," Daniel said evenly, "we'd like to talk."

"Talk or talk?" Ryan asked, wiggling his eyebrows.

Izzy raised a hand. "I swear if you add air quotes one more time today…"

Daniel jumped in before the bickering became an Olympic sport. "We just wanted to tell you both that we're trying. Officially. Izzy and me."

Freddy gave his signature eyebrow lift, looking between them like he was both impressed and annoyed that he hadn't been given earlier intel.

Ryan was mid-bite and gave a loud mmm of satisfaction that could've been either croissant-related or love-declaration-related. Hard to say.

"So," Ryan said, swallowing dramatically, "this is your big reveal? You're dating again? My guy, I thought you were going to tell us you'd bought a goat farm or joined an underground poetry cult."

"I'd join that," Freddy said absently. "Depends on the benefits."

"Can I finish?" Daniel asked, shooting them both a look.

"Fine," Ryan said, leaning forward, resting his chin on his knuckles like a gossip columnist. "Tell us how you rode off into the mist."

Daniel hesitated, but Izzy nudged him gently.

"I needed time," Daniel admitted. "To think. About everything. Sandra. My past. Where I've gone wrong. But I realised I was scared. Of happiness. And I didn't want to be anymore."

Freddy looked serious now. "So, what changed?"

"Izzy did," Daniel said simply. "She makes me want to stay. Not run."

Ryan sniffed and fanned his eyes dramatically. "Okay, stop. If you two make me feel emotions again, I'm going to need wine and Enya."

Izzy chuckled. "It's 11 in the morning."

"Which is late in Europe," Ryan declared. "And time is a construct when love is in the room!"

Daniel was exasperated.

"What the hell is an Enya?" Daniel asked.

Ryan chuckled. "Daniel, you ARE an old man. Enya is an Irish singer and composer. With an estimated equivalent of over 90 million album sales worldwide, Enya is the bestselling Irish solo artist, and the second bestselling music act from Ireland overall—after the rock band U2."

Daniel looked at Ryan and was about to say something when Freddy interjected. "Daniel, I just want her to be happy. If you're in—really in—then I'm good. But if you hurt her, I have creative ways of making you regret it. Ever heard of a reverse espresso shot?"

Ryan perked up. "Oh, do you mean when you inject hot coffee upward? I read about that once in a war novel."

"Can we not talk about coffee torture while I'm trying to build something sacred?" Daniel asked.

"Okay, okay," Ryan said, hands up. "But you better let me plan something. I don't care if it's a first date do-over or a commitment ceremony in a grocery store. Give me this."

Freddy shook his head. "He's your problem now."

"I've always been his problem," Ryan whispered to Izzy like they were in a spy thriller.

Daniel leaned over and gently took Izzy's hand, grounding her. She looked over at him and felt it, that quiet warmth. That certainty.

Ryan's antics aside, this felt real. It was real.

"Well," Freddy said, standing and stretching, "I'll leave you two lovebirds to whatever it is people in their 60 do after emotional declarations and croissants. Scrapbooking?"

"Freddy, we ARE not in our 60s!" screamed Izzy.

Ryan leapt up. "Do not diss scrapbooking. That's where memories go to live forever."

"Freddy," Izzy said, standing too, "thank you. Really."

He pulled her in for a one-armed hug. "I'll always have your back, Izzy."

Daniel approached and extended his hand.

Freddy took it after a brief pause. "Don't screw this up, Carter."

"Not planning to."

Ryan clapped his hands. "Group hug? Too soon?"

"Nope," Izzy and Daniel said at the same time.

Ryan launched in like a puppy. The hug was lopsided, weird, and slightly too long. But none of them let go first.

Eventually, Freddy peeled away and reached for his keys. "I've got a lunch to prep for. Try not to emotionally combust before 1 p.m."

Ryan followed him out but stopped at the door. "I'm going to text you 17 ship name ideas so you can have your scarves embroidered."

"No," Izzy warned.

"I'm leaning toward Dizzy," Ryan said, then dashed out before they could throw anything at him.

Suddenly Freddy stuck his head before Ryan could close the door. "Izzy, have you told Mum what's happening yet?"

"No."

"Oh, that is going to be good. See ya, sis."

Alone at last, Daniel and Izzy sat down on the couch again.

"I don't know what we just survived," Daniel said, rubbing his face.

"I think it was a friendship cyclone," Izzy murmured.

"But a loving one," he added.

Izzy looked over at him, warmth rising like steam from tea. "You handled Freddy well."

"I think I passed the sibling test."

"You did."

Daniel leaned back, relaxed now. "Still think we need to prepare for your mother, though."

Izzy groaned. "Oh, that's an entirely different emotional hurricane."

"Ryan's going to want in on that, isn't he?"

Izzy nodded. "We should probably warn her."

Daniel smiled. "For now, let's just enjoy this quiet moment first."

22

A Visit to Maman

Izzy

There's a very specific kind of dread one felt when calling their mother to announce a visit. Multiply that by ten when the mother in question was a French national who once told off a Catholic priest for speaking too softly during mass.

And multiply that by infinity when you were bringing Daniel, the man you might love, and Ryan, the human equivalent of a golden retriever who found a case of wine.

I called Maman around 3 p.m. on a Thursday.

"Isabelle?" she answered in her thick accent, the 's' pronounced like a snake coiled in velvet.

"Hi, Maman," I said, already wincing. "I'm coming up this weekend."

"You are? What's wrong? Are you sick? Is Freddy sick? Who died?"

"No one! We're fine. Freddy's coming too. And we're bringing guests."

There was a beat of silence.

"Guests?"

"Yes."

"Izzy."

"Yes?"

"Are you bringing a man?"

Technically yes, I thought. But I smiled like she could see it. "Maybe. You'll see."

"Hmm."

The 'hmm' lasted five seconds. I knew because I counted. That was her judgment-telegraphing sound. A sonic eyebrow rising like a SpaceX ship to the sky.

"We'll be there Saturday."

"I will prepare roast chicken," she said flatly. "Not because I approve. Because I am polite."

I'd never really told Daniel about Maman.

She lived in Mermaid Beach on the Gold Coast, up in Queensland. Marguerite Isabelle Josephine Laurant was 73 years old, having married Monsieur Frédéric André Laurant at the tender age of 18 years.

Monsieur Laurant had had the misfortunate of getting caught with the wife of a retired police commissioner in Paris flagrante delicto and was rewarded with three bullets to the heart, leaving young Marguerite Isabelle Josephine Laurant a widow at the young age of 23 with two young children but a massive $135 million Swiss franc fortune. One she invested over the years and, after making sure her children were raised to take care of themselves, she moved to, what was then, a quaint little chateau on Mermaid Beach now worth a bit over $25 million Australian.

Chateau Laurant was one kilometre from its private beach. It was aggressively cultivated and taken care by a staff of 12, which Mamam supervised like a drilled sergeant.

When they landed at the airport, there were two starched limos waiting for them. Izzy went into explanation mode. "Daniel, Ryan. I never really shared with you about…Maman. She is a bit special and has some funds behind her."

"Some funds? Enough to hire two limos to pick us up?" Ryan added.

"Not exactly…" stated Freddy. "She owns these two limos and one more."

Daniel and Ryan looked at each other. "How many does she have?"

Izzy just said, "You both will see when we get there. Don't fret. It is not a big thing."

As they got into the first limo (the second one they were told was to carry their suitcases) Daniel felt underdressed. He was dressed nicely in a button-down shirt, clean jeans, and nervous sweat. Ryan was wearing a flamingo patterned Hawaiian shirt.

"I don't think your mum's going to like me," Ryan said cheerfully.

"She already doesn't like you," I muttered. "She doesn't know you exist yet, but somehow she knows she disapproves."

"Excellent," Ryan said. "Better to go in low and surprise them."

"Please don't talk about yourself like an underperforming mutual fund," Daniel muttered.

"Hey, if she's French, I've got this. I once dated a pastry chef named Claudine. I'll charm her like a fresh baguette."

Freddy snorted. "And end up toasted."

Maman greeted us on the portico in a crisp linen blouse, her hair twisted up in a regal bun. Her eyes skimmed Daniel with suspicion, passed over Freddy with relief and a quick peck, and landed on Ryan like he'd tracked mud onto her carpet from three suburbs over.

"You must be Freddy's friend?" she said, extending her hand to Daniel.

"No, ma'am," Daniel replied. "I'm with Izzy."

"You are?"

"Yes."

"Hm." She turned to Ryan. "And this is?"

"Ryan Michaels," he said, giving her a deep, theatrical bow. "Part-time academic, full-time delight."

"Ah," she said, withdrawing her hand. "A clown."

Ryan blinked. "Technically, that's my middle name."

It was time for lunch.

The table was beautifully set. White cloth, wine glasses, fine China and two roasted chickens. So perfectly roasted it looked like a food stylist had painted them. Maman dismissed her servants and served each of us, saying our names aloud like she was stamping passports.

"Freddy."

"Merci, Maman."

"Isabelle."

"Merci."

"Daniel."

"Thank you, ma'am."

"Ryan."

"Delighted, madame."

"No wine for you."

Ryan's mouth opened. Closed. "Noted."

Lunch was, in a word, tense.

Maman grilled Daniel like he was a steak she didn't ask for.

Where he was from?

Why he got divorced?

Why hadn't he cut his hair differently?

What is his credit score?

"You are a consultant—is that not someone between jobs?"

Daniel, to his credit, held firm.

But when she asked why he hadn't called her before dating her daughter, something in him snapped.

"With all due respect, Madame Laurant," Daniel said, setting down his wineglass, "I wasn't aware I needed clearance. Izzy is an adult. And she's more than capable of choosing who's right for her."

There was silence.

Utter, holy, silence.

Even Freddy paused mid-chew.

Maman's eyes narrowed.

Ryan whispered to Freddy, "He's dead."

But then Maman leaned back. A slow smile curved on her lips.

"Enfin," she said. "Someone with a spine."

She lifted her wineglass. "Bienvenue, Daniel."

Daniel blinked. "Wait? What?"

She shrugged. "I had to know. Izzy likes soft men. Dreamers. I had to see if you had teeth. You do. I approve. For now."

After lunch, we all walked through her massive garden. Ryan tried to name every flower. He got three wrong, one of them so badly that the geraniums are still offended.

Maman looped her arm through mine.

"He is interesting," she said, nodding toward Daniel. "Quiet, but not weak. I like that. But the other one…"

"Ryan?"

"I would like to throw him into the ocean."

"I think he'd float," I offered.

"Like a bloated duck," she muttered. "Tell me, do you love this, Daniel?"

"I do," I said honestly.

"Then make sure he knows. Men forget. Especially when they're happy. It's the misery that makes them remember what they have."

"Very uplifting, Maman."

"It's not my job to be uplifting. It's my job to protect your heart. But I will admit, this one may be good for you."

Back at the chateau, Ryan came out of the guest bathroom wearing a robe that clearly belonged to Maman.

"Don't ask," Freddy said, shaking his head.

Maman walked by and saw him. "You are using my lavender robe?"

"It's plush!" Ryan said, spinning.

"It was from my honeymoon."

"I will treat it with the respect of a thousand lavender fields."

"Put it back before I light it on fire."

The next two days flew. We had more roasted chicken lunches but plenty of wine (except for Ryan) and had many moments of private talk with Izzy and her Maman while Freddy and Ryan were at the beach.

As we drove away in the limo to catch our plane back to Sydney, Daniel looked over at me. "She's intense."

"She is. But you handled her."

"I talked back. That could've gone sideways."

"You talked back respectfully. That's the only way through the gauntlet."

In the back seat, Ryan sighed deeply. "I think she wanted to kill me."

"She did," Freddy said. "But she'll never forget you."

Ryan grinned. "My work here is done."

And so, with the lavender-scented robe terror behind us and her unlikely approval earned, the next chapter of our story had begun.

Not with a dramatic gesture or whispered promises, but several roast chicken lunches, a French matriarch, and the kind of courage that only came when you realised the person you were fighting for was worth every awkward moment.

23

Eyes Wide Open

It had been several months since that fateful weekend in Queensland, where roast chicken and lavender-scented disapproval somehow forged a final bond. Now, life for Daniel and Izzy had found its rhythm, not flashy or perfect, but real. That kind of soft, satisfying real that creeps up on you and whispers: This is it. This is the thing.

Izzy had made some big decisions in those months.

The Velvet Note, her passion, and burden, had evolved into a thriving jazz haven run by more than just her steam and will. Freddy, her fiercely loyal and endlessly competent brother, had finally accepted her offer to take over as general manager.

"You mean I get to yell at the vendors and not feel guilty about it?" he'd asked with a grin. "Sign me up."

Together, they brought in a night shift manager to take care of the late crowds, and even promoted Beatrix to day manager, which made Beatrix cry into her soy latte before immediately organizing a colour-coded calendar for the next six months.

Izzy felt lighter now.

She had time for her life, for Daniel, for slow mornings and actual weekends. The Velvet Note was still hers, but she no longer had to carry it like an anvil strapped to her chest.

Daniel had undergone his own transformation.

He wrapped up several consulting jobs, one of which turned out to be a dream project for a literary startup that wanted long-term strategy help but only needed him for about 20 hours a week. It paid well, respected his time, and left him space to finally do what had haunted him for years: finish his novel.

"You mean the one with the talking dog that moonlights as a jazz pianist?" Izzy teased one night as they curled up in bed.

"That was a phase," he replied dryly. "It evolved. Now the dog is a therapist."

Ryan, of course, remained an unavoidable fixture in their lives. And in a plot twist that neither of them could have written, Marguerite Isabelle Josephine Laurant had taken an extremely specific liking to him.

At first, it was baffling. Marguerite invited Ryan to the chateau for wine tastings, obscure cheese tastings, and once, a lesson in fencing.

"She called me l'idiot at least six times," Ryan said proudly. "I think that means she likes me."

"Or she's warning the villagers," Daniel muttered.

"She told me I had le je ne sais quoi," Ryan added with a dramatic flourish.

"She meant you're a mystery she hasn't solved yet."

"Exactly."

Still, it worked.

Somehow, impossibly, Ryan's brand of chaotic charm slotted into Marguerite's calculated world. They bickered like a spin-off show no one had asked for, but everyone secretly loved.

Izzy didn't question it anymore. Her mum just made sure the guest room was always clean and stocked with Ryan's preferred tea.

As for the two of them, Izzy and Daniel, their life was a patchwork of normal and new. Breakfasts shared, notes scribbled on napkins, afternoons spent reading or walking along Sydney harbour and a few trips to the cabin, just them.

There were still moments of doubt, of course.

No one lived through heartbreak without scars.

But the thing they kept choosing, every day, was each other.

One Tuesday evening, they are chatting at The Velvet Note, tucked into their favourite booth under the old Coltrane poster. Freddy was behind the bar, humming something vaguely familiar and bluesy. The new night manager, Rhea, was taking over from Beatrix, while a baby faced singer nervously adjusted his mic.

At the table near the stage, a young couple was arguing. Not angry, but with the sort of half-whispered, wide-eyed tension of two people trying to figure out if they should break up or finally take the leap.

Izzy watched them for a while, her head resting on Daniel's shoulder.

He nudged her gently. "That was us, once."

"Was it?"

"Well, I didn't look that young," he admitted. "And you definitely argued better."

She laughed. "I still do."

They sat in companionable silence for a beat, the clink of glasses and the low hum of music wrapping around them like a blanket.

"You know what I love about this?" Daniel said finally.

"My overpriced coffee and cocktails?"

"That we get to do it differently. Not perfect. Not movie-worthy. Just us."

Izzy looked over at him, her eyes soft. "You mean grown-up love."

"Exactly. The boring, beautiful kind."

They clinked their glasses. Izzy took a sip, then smiled.

"We should tell that young couple not to bother with the drama. Just skip to the good stuff."

"We could," Daniel said, leaning back. "But then they wouldn't earn it."

They watched a while longer as the couple fell quiet, fingers inching toward each other across the table.

Izzy turned to Daniel. "We've come far, haven't we?"

"Yes, we have."

And that was how it ended.

Not with fireworks or sweeping declarations, but with two people choosing each other again and again.

Over toast.

Over mistakes.

Over corny statements.

Over Tuesday night, jazz, and quiet realisation.

Love, at their age, wasn't about dramatic gestures or fairy tales. It was about choosing each other every day, with eyes wide open.

About The Author

Flung into one of life's most daunting challenges at just 11 years old, José's journey began in Havana, Cuba. The Cuban Revolution uprooted his family, forcing his parents to make a heart-wrenching decision: send him away, alone, to safety. José boarded a plane, uncertain of what lay ahead, and landed not in the comfort of familiar faces but at an orphanage in a small Georgia town called Washington.

For the next seven years, he navigated life as a stranger in a foreign land. Letters were few, and the hope of reuniting with his parents became a distant dream.

Finally, at 18—now a high school graduate in Atlanta—he embraced his family once again. The reunion was bittersweet, for José had grown up without them, becoming independent far sooner than most.

Determined to carve out a life for himself, José pursued a degree in Business Administration at Georgia State University. He stepped into the world of finance, starting at First National Bank of Atlanta (now Wells Fargo). His natural talent for numbers and strategic thinking propelled him to become a project manager in financial consulting, leading to high-stakes ventures. His career took him across the globe, from bustling cities in the United States to financial hubs in Europe and even the sunburnt coasts of Australia.

It was in Camden, New South Wales, that a new chapter of José's life began. While exploring the quiet rhythms of this Australian town, José stumbled upon a local writers' group. What began as a casual interest soon grew into an unquenchable passion. The stories swirling in his mind took shape, and from that creative spark, Danny Monk, his first major character, was born—a mischievous, intriguing figure who captured the complexities José had observed throughout his life. Writing Danny's story was a revelation, and with that, José discovered a new calling.

Fast forward to today. José is not just a writer but a prolific storyteller, balancing multiple projects at once. He is deep into his seventh short story collection while simultaneously crafting his latest work—a crime novel slated for release in 2026. His books, filled with engaging characters and complex narratives, reflect a life rich with experiences, challenges, and triumphs.

Yet José's world is not confined to the keyboard and screen. Inspiration comes from everywhere, and one of his favourite pastimes is to wander the local mall, quietly observing people, noting quirks, behaviours, and snippets of conversation that might spark a new character or plot twist. When he's not writing or gathering ideas, José immerses himself in literature, feeding his mind with the words of others.

Outside of his creative pursuits, José treasures the simple pleasures of life—particularly long walks with his wife, Miriam, through the scenic streets of Spring Farm. Their leisurely strolls are a cherished routine; moments of reflection where stories, memories, and dreams intertwine.

José's life is a tapestry woven from adversity, perseverance, and creativity. From the orphanage in Georgia to the financial districts of the world, and now to the quiet corners of Spring Farm, where stories are born, his journey is a testament to the resilience of the human spirit. And with each book he writes, José not only tells stories but also leaves behind pieces of himself, enriching the lives of readers across the globe.

José F. Nodar © 2025

Other books by José F. Nodar

English

- Books, Pens & Larceny

- Mending Hearts at Crystal Cove

- A Love Finally Spoken

- The Legacy Compass

- The Universe Between Us

- The Time Bus

- SEX

- Stories to Share with My Partner Book 1

- Stories to Share with My Partner Book 2

- Stories to Share with My Partner Book 3

- Stories to Share with My Partner Book 4

- Stories to Share with My Partner Book 5

- Stories to Share with My Partner Book 6

- Stories to Share with My Partner Book 7

- Stories to Share with My Partner Book 8

- Stories to Share with My Partner Book 9

Spanish

- Cuentos Para Compartir con Mi Pareja Libro 1

- Cuentos Para Compartir con Mi Pareja Libro 2

- Cuentos Para Compartir con Mi Pareja Libro 3

- Libros, Bolígrafos y Hurto

- Reparando Corazones en Crystal Cove

- El Autobús del Tiempo

www.ingramcontent.com/pod-product-compliance
Lightning Source LLC
Chambersburg PA
CBHW040537170726
48295CB00012B/497